**Fintr**

...**ax.com**

*Adding value to your transactions*

Sarah

Tax Free Shopping

Multicurrency Credit Card Processing

PREMIER
ELECTRUM

Gift Card

C000110796

# Danny and Clare Are Splitting Up

The publishers are grateful to the following for permission to reproduce copyright material:

BMG Music Publishing Ltd. for lyrics from 'Everybody Knows' by The Divine Comedy.

Lyrics from 'My Sharona': Words and Music by Douglas Lars Fieger/Berton Averre © 1998 Eighties Music/Small Hill Music, Rondor Music (London) Ltd, SW6 4TW. Reproduced by permission of IMP Ltd.

First published in 1998 by
Marino Books
an imprint of Mercier Press
16 Hume Street Dublin 2
Tel: (01) 661 5299; Fax: (01) 661 8583
E.mail: books@marino.ie

Trade enquiries to CMD Distribution
55A Spruce Avenue
Stillorgan Industrial Park
Blackrock County Dublin
Tel: (01) 294 2556; Fax: (01) 294 2564

© Frank Coughlan 1998

ISBN 1 85635 077 6

10 9 8 7 6 5 4 3 2 1

A CIP record for this title is available
from the British Library

Cover image © Stockbyte™
Cover design by Penhouse Design
Printed in Ireland by ColourBooks,
Baldoyle Industrial Estate, Dublin 13

# Danny and Clare Are Splitting Up

## Frank Coughlan

Thanks to Deb, Jo O'Donoghue, Anne O'Donnell, Aongus Collins, Christy Ward,  Cormac Deane, Liam Mulcahy and Linda Kenny

*In memory of my mother and father*

# I

## (DUBLIN – NOW)

Move! It's easy. Handbrake off. Clutch. Indicator. Jesus wept.

I flash him. Again. And again. Nothing. Now the lights have gone red and the old tosser still hasn't edged an inch. I can just about make out the back of his little bald head peeping out over the driver's seat and his bony fingers grimly clutching the steering wheel at ten to two.

Why didn't the senile bastard use his bus pass? Or maybe he's not senile at all. Maybe he's deliberately acting the geriatric, just to piss me off.

If he doesn't move his spluttering heap sharpish, I'll ram him right up the backside. Wallop. Grandad or no grandad. Geriatric or not.

Not that I'm in a hurry to get anywhere special. More in a hurry to get away from somewhere. House and home, to be precise.

It hasn't all been my fault, some would say none of it. But it has being coming for a long time. Tonight just happened to be that time. I eyeballed her, pressed my face to hers and screamed it so loud that I could just about make out my own words.

She was frightened and crying and then not crying

and shouting back. I must have been crying too because I can see from the rear view mirror that my face is puffy. It's red, taut and it feels really hot, as if I had a fever.

I can't remember my exact words. But I suspect that Matt, who scurried off to his bedroom terrified, will remember the entire episode, frame by frame, for the rest of his life. He must have heard me tell her I was going. Not coming back. That I really hated her. Her face. Her lies. Her life. Our life. Our marriage.

I pushed past her and ran upstairs, found my old kit bag and tossed whatever came to hand into it. Then I charged back down, grabbed my ciggies, my coat and car keys from the hall table and left. A final glare and slam.

Matt was peeping out from behind his bedroom curtain, but I pretended not to see. I didn't want to see. Couldn't bear to.

A year ago, the three of us would have spent an autumn evening like this strolling along the beach. Now Clare and I don't talk, except to exchange idle chatter and worthless piffle. When things that needed to be said got said tonight, we reduced each other to ashes within minutes.

Then I did what exactly what I had threatened to do. And what I knew was inevitable – I took a walk, possibly the longest walk of my life.

My hands are still shaking and I'm angrier than I've ever been. About 200 per cent angrier. The crock in front is still belching purple fumes but it seems anxious to be off, perhaps finally sussing that the man in the Beetle is having a bad day and is not to be messed with.

I hope I didn't hit Clare. Pray to God I didn't. Never have. Never would. But did I? I did push her against the kitchen wall, prodded her with a finger. I can see now why she was so scared. I really must have lost it. I scan the pavement for a phone box. I should ring her. Not to say sorry, just see if she's all right. But I can't. I shouldn't. Why should I?

I take a deep breath. The sort that Clare's always telling me to take, but which I never have. In. Deep. Out. Slowly. And again.

A car beeps politely from behind and I concentrate to find that the only thing left of grandad is a long toxic trail. Christ. I raise a hand in apology. Then I stall. I never stall. My yellow Beetle never stalls. But we have now. I'm in bits.

If walking out on a marriage is this gut-wrenching, I don't want to have to do it again. I better make it count this time. This is the real thing. Lights. Camera. Action.

I give the car a rev, indicate left and decide to head for Peter's place in Milltown. I'll ask him for political asylum and a cold beer. He'll give me both.

# 2

## (Cork – Then)

'So what's your name?'

'I've already told you. You *are* pissed'

I am, of course, but I'll make an effort anyway and I try hard to remember. She's very cute, this girl, and chatting her up for a while will help idle away the minutes as we wait outside the rugby club disco.

'Your name is Clare. Clare Fitz-something or other. You're a friend of that lanky weirdo from Grange. So there now.'

I knew them both vaguely, just to see. They're like inseparable twins, although not identical – not by a long shot. Clare's pretty. Definitely pretty. Her friend is definitely not. More a freak of nature and fashion, like the ugly sister the Frankenstein monster didn't like to talk about. And probably into Frank Zappa or astrology or some such bollox.

Clare's face, which moments earlier was a picture of mere indifference, now throws me a look that could maim a sensitive soul for life.

I stand there weaving gently from side to side, my hands dug into my pockets jangling change, and I try to work out what it is I've said. Then it dawns. Maybe suggesting that her bosom buddy was so strange that even the tide wouldn't take her out was a bit iffy. Shite. Shit.

Before I have chance to compose a retraction, she turns her head away and drags her fashionably tattered denim jacket across her chest as if to ward off a gust of biting wind. But there is none, so it must be to ward off me instead.

Clare can't do much more without losing her place in the queue that she's patiently stood in for over an hour. I swaggered along five minutes ago, making a point of jumping the line. Nobody protested. Somebody must have twigged I was with Jimmy. And Jimmy Flynn is mad. Too mad and too unpredictable to meddle with.

A blast of stale, recycled air and the distinctive sound of Mott the Hoople drifts over us as the bouncers, a couple of prop-forwards on security duty, push open the doors to let another straggling stream of teenagers in.

A boisterous bunch of drunk lads scrum down and charge from behind, causing a mighty heave and an ear-battering roar. We're carried away in an avalanche of bodies to the door.

Clare loses her footing, stumbles and instinctively grabs me by the sleeve and I catch her by the waist and haul her through the door after me. She's immediately cross with herself but smiles a tight, pert little smile nonetheless.

'Thanks. Thought I was a goner for a horrible second,' she says, looking at me quickly, coyly, before turning on her heels. I must be forgiven.

I can see that she has the legend Thin Lizzy sewn on to the back of her jacket, but the second 'z' is only a stitch or two away from coming undone. It probably happened in the crush. She doesn't seem like the sort of girl who'd head out on a Saturday night being deliberately blasphemous.

I wonder for a second whether I should go after her and tell her, but she has already been swallowed up by a sweaty mass of bodies on the dance floor. She's nice though. Pretty. Kind of dainty, petite, or whatever.

I dig deeply and furtively into my combat jacket for the entrance money and I count it out slowly. Once, then again and then a third time. I have just enough to get in – just – but I should have more. I try to work out how many vodkas and lime I had. Too bloody many.

I don't feel too clever now, all that fuss at the door. My head is light. Detachable. I pay up but don't wait for my ticket and bolt for the toilets, which are as far away as they possibly could be and still be in the same pavilion.

I make them. Almost. My stomach heaves and I throw up. Loudly and often and everywhere, even over my runners and some guy's jeans. I wipe my shirt with one hand and extend the other while muttering a sincere, but garbled, apology. He's too appalled to say anything, but his girlfriend puts it succinctly enough. I'm a retard, seemingly.

By the time my stomach has organised a second sortie I have my head down a toilet bowl. Safest place. I think they're playing Deep Purple somewhere.

I drench my head under the cold tap and rinse my mouth out. Rejuvenated, I elbow and weave my way onto the dance floor and submerge into a kaleidoscopic sea of red, blue and yellow flashing lights. Yes, it's definitely Deep Purple. Something from *Made In Japan* but I can't put a name on it. Brilliant. Magic.

I catch sight of Jimmy, his great mane of curly hair following him as he crisscrosses the floor. He's whacking lumps out of his air guitar and is as drunk as a lord.

Jimmy has a hip flask of brandy; he showed me it earlier. He nicked it from his old fella's good Crombie after the inter-pro between Munster and Leinster. His da played for Ireland in the fifties and now Jimmy says he drinks for his country instead. Nothing wrong with that, not in my book anyway. Better than a craw-thumping old misery like mine.

Somebody climbs on my back, covers my face with outsize hands and drags me to the ground. Jimmy, of course. Now he's kneeling on me, clattering the back of my head and screaming the words of the song. He really is twisted tonight. I just hope all the brandy isn't gone.

'Getttoffmee, ya crazy bastard, Flynnie,' I roar, kicking wildly.

I pretend I'm mad as anything, because I know everyone is watching, with only those on the fringes of the dance floor still bopping. I could get skulled alone on the buzz that goes with being Jimmy's best mate. Straight guy and funny guy. Lennon and McCartney. Charlton and Law. Butch Cassidy and the Sundance Kid. That sort of vibe anyway.

He drags me up by the back of the shirt and produces the flask with a great theatrical flourish.

'I kept the last slug for you, Danny, my man. It's like diesel but it's fucking lethal all the same.'

I throw it down my neck. One gulp . . . two . . . three. Mother of Divine Fuck, the flask was half-full. My throat is ablaze and some of it runs down my shirt, I can even feel it trickle down to the small of my back.

I toss the empty flask in the air and catch it, hug it and

then drop kick it towards the far end where the disc jockey is. Jimmy roars the impromptu commentary.

'It's an up-and-under – and Ireland are charging the England twenty-five . . . '

We both bundle forward, barging and shouldering our way to the top corner of the hall. He lunges at me and I manage to wriggle free but I trip myself up and we both end up a tangled heap on the floor.

I'm dizzy now and the room spins about me as it does for town drunks in B-movies. Like it did for Lee Marvin in *Cat Ballou*. We laugh ourselves hoarse, then Jimmy remembers the flask and gathers himself up and goes hunting for it.

I close my eyes, wait, and then gingerly open them again. The room is standing perfectly still now, but I don't think I can stand up yet. I blink, close them and open them again. Now Clare Fitz is standing there, looking down at me and laughing.

'It's you,' I say with commendable accuracy and sounding surprised.

She shakes her head in disbelief.

'You are one mad bastard. Actually, you and Jimmy Flynn are two mad bastards. Can you get up?

'Course I can.'

And I do. Very carefully, dusting myself down and pulling a piece of chewing gum from the seat of my jeans. My new jeans too. Shit.

I'm rightly pissed all right. Very, very. But from a tiny, sealed compartment of my brain that seems immune to the effects of alcoholic over-indulgence, a tiny voice pleads with me to pick over my words carefully before letting them spill out this time. I have just enough sense to pay heed.

I nearly topple but she steadies me by placing one hand on my upper arm and the other under my elbow, like a nurse might. The place is pounding to Thin Lizzy now and the crowd swarms the floor.

This new DJ is good, so bloody good he'll never last. The floor is bouncing, trying to anticipate the next surge and lurch. I remember that Lizzy are Clare's band, because her jacket declares as much.

I drape a heavy arm over her shoulder and ask her would she like to dance but she promptly removes it, laughs and tells me that I need air. She points me towards the exit sign and gives me a gentle shove.

'See ya,' she roars over the din and gives me a very final sort of wave.

She's bopping with her friend now and has her back to me. My eyes, which shrewdly search out skirt even on nights when the rest of me is incapable of chasing it, fall on her neat little rear.

Weirdo notices and throws a well-practised look of contempt in my direction and then concentrates on wriggling her substantial jugs every which way. If I knew her better I'd tell her that her tits had no rhythm. That would be gas.

The shutters are coming down on my brain but I walk towards the exit because I was told to and because the bracing September night air tumbling through it seems as vital to me now as a drink of water to Lawrence of Arabia. Great film that. Peter O'Toole. Magic.

As I stumble up the last few steps, a rhino of a man, whom I know simply as Jumbo and who still togs out for the club's third team at forty-plus, pins me up against the wall and wags a disfigured finger in my face.

'We're watching you, boy. You and that young buck Flynn are riding your luck lately. We've had complaints. How old are you?

'Seventeen. Born sixteenth of the twelfth, 1957. Sirrrrrrr!'

I try to click my heels together and salute. He ignores this and just prods me with his ugly paw again.

'Seventeen? Look at you. You're out of your tree. What's your name?'

'Daniel F. – for Francis – Hayes. Siirrrrr!' Click.

'Now Danny boy, fuck off out of here and don't ever turn up in that state again. Go home and sleep it off.'

He grabs me by the scruff of the neck and twirls me around.

'March, Private Hayes,' he shouts, making my little joke his own now, 'hup, two, three, four . . . '

He lets go and I'm propelled down the entrance steps. I try to keep my balance but I crash on to the tarmac, scrape my wrist and whack my ankle against the wing of a Cortina. The pain of it rallies my numbed senses long enough for me to direct a tirade of abuse at the swinging door.

'Piss off you too, you ugly, fascist pillock!' I scream, 'I was leaving anyway.'

A small sprinkling of stragglers and smoochers look at me with a mixture of amusement and, I'd imagine, disgust, as I hobble out of the carpark, but I don't care. They're all fascists too. All I want to do now is lie down. And sleep.

Someone has started to clatter me across the face. There's a voice involved too, which I eventually figure out belongs to Jimmy.

'Wake up, Danny, for Jasus sake.'

He's yelling into my ear from a distance of three inches.

Slap . . .

'It's time to go home . . . '

Slap . . .

' . . . you're in some state, come on.'

Slap!

He sits me up and I open my eyes, grin in a sort of lopsided way while wiping saliva from my mouth. I'm in Seat 23, Row F of the club stand. Beats me.

I'm less drunk now, but what promises to be one bitch of a hangover is just starting to pitch its tent in my head. It shouldn't arrive till sun-up but my little impromptu two-hour nap – I was comatose, really – has fooled it into clocking in early.

I'd forgotten about my military manoeuvres with Jumbo but my ankle is simply aching to remind me. I tell Jimmy all about it as we feel our way gingerly down the steps in the black dark. By the time we reach the road I manage to reassert my independence. It's not too sore now and I begin to walk it off. I won't sue this time.

Buttoned up against the drizzle that has just begun to sneak down, we set about our mile walk home. I'll have to take it slowly.

'Clare whatshername told me you'd be outside,' Jimmy says, lighting a cigarette first for me and then himself. 'Think she has the hots for you.'

'I wish.'

'You not think so? Seemed very concerned. Thinks we're both lunatics and some girls like that. They might end up marrying little career shits. But they like to get inside the undies of a few nutters first.'

'Not her. She seems very sane to me. Nice kinda.'

Jimmy hugs me to him. Strong bastard. All that rugby, I suppose. That's why girls are always begging him for it, I reckon. They like all that manly stuff. Always have, always will.

'Look,' he says, 'Stevie Keane – you know, the mad bastard who plays on the wing for my crowd – went out with her once and he told me she's a bit of a goer.'

He tapped the side of his nose twice with a finger, nearly missing the second time. 'Mum's the word.'

I didn't know whether to be intimidated or encouraged by this revelation. But I nodded gravely anyway and changed the subject.

'Did you find the flask?'

'I did, eventually. I'll sneak it back into the old man's coat tonight. And wait for a refill. Great stuff, wasn't it?'

'Great stuff, great night. Fucking great.'

Jimmy goes his own way, humming that syrupy ballad 'Clare' for my benefit. But this piss-take doesn't sift through my tired and soaked brain until he's a mere silhouetted speck in the middle distance, spotlighted by the glow of a streetlight above him.

I think about shouting something clever, but nothing comes. Instead, I set my face against the drizzle that has quickly matured into a downpour and limp left for home. I promise myself to ask this Clare bird out soon. Definitely by next weekend.

But I know from experience that the promises I make to myself when I'm drunk are rarely fulfilled. This one is different though. I promise.

# 3

## (DUBLIN)

Peter has been a real brick. Just like you'd expect a good mate who goes way back to be. When I turned up at his door like a stray dog, he said all the right things. That is, he said next to nothing, only to ask did I want a can, or something stronger, and to tell me where I'd find the duvet.

We watched some Spanish footie on EuroSport into the early hours, only because we both knew that if I went to bed I'd not sleep. Silence and darkness would provide the perfect backdrop for an endless replay of the evening's traumatic events.

Later, rolling an empty Bud between the palms of his hands and studying the rug as if it was the first time he'd ever laid eyes on it, he said he'd listen all night if I wanted to talk or he'd get lost and go to bed if I didn't. So we had another few beers and I talked and he listened. I veered from the incoherent to the rambling and back again. But he just nodded.

Peter isn't around the place much and he says I'm welcome to stay put until the dust has settled. He's single and works hard at staying that way. Many women have woken up in his bedroom once, but very few twice. Smart lad.

The following evening I orbited the phone for ever before picking it up and ringing Clare. The last time I had been that nervous on the blower was when I phoned her for that first date twenty-two years ago. Imagine that – twenty-two years. To the week, almost. But there was no giggling or flirting this time. As if anticipating my call, Clare's voice was ice itself.

'Hello?'

'Clare, it's me.'

Silence. A long silence, the sort of one that says more than hundreds of carelessly chosen words. We've spent hours in rooms together lately with silences that lasted much longer, but this was the silence that said it all.

'Are you there?'

A long weary sigh. 'Yes. What do you want?'

'Well, we should talk.' I sounded like some jerk in a bad soap. But maybe that was apt too, seeing as my life was turning into one.

'Talk? With you? You mean get slapped about by you . . .'

'I never laid as much as a finger . . .'

I could feel the anger rise in me. And panic too.

'Oh, what a selective memory you have, you little shit. You're honestly trying to tell me that you can't remember banging your wife's head against a fucking brick wall hardly twenty-four hours ago?'

Strong language for a teacher. Even this one. I had to sit down. My mouth had gone completely dry and I needed both hands to steady the mouthpiece.

'Don't. Please, Clare, stop this. What if Matt hears you . . . ?'

She cut me short.

'Matt's in Cork with his granny. I took him out of school. A few missed classes at ten years of age won't harm him. Less harm than being around this marriage anyway. He won't be back until Sunday.'

That led us into the next silence and after an eternity I asked if Saturday afternoon was a good time to call over to collect some stuff. She sounded tired then. Weary. That brief blinding flash of anger was gone and she muttered that, yes, that it would be fine. Then she put the phone down.

I cradled mine a while longer and I could hear myself cry before I realised that I was. Then I could taste the salt of my tears and I wondered if she was crying too.

I could try to convince myself that since that phone call I've started to get on top of it, except that I don't have the energy for self-deception. Calling out to the house this weekend will tell a lot.

At least I'm sleeping a little and it takes time to get used to sleeping in a strange bed and on your own. Even during the worst of it, when we only exchanged pleasantries for Matt's sake, I could always depend on Clare for body warmth.

Sometimes when she'd fall asleep, Clare would instinctively snuggle up to my back and tuck her knees in behind mine. But she didn't like to make love, not with me at any rate. I only found out about her affair with Him in January, although they were going at it hammer and tongs long before then. She bought me the Beatles' *Anthology III* for Christmas. He got a collection of erotic verse.

I know, because I came across it tucked away in the corner of a wardrobe. I naively thought it was for me but I never got it. It's seems so obvious now, just a case of elementary deduction. I didn't think anything of it at the time.

He's a primary teacher too, somewhere out on the northside, and they met at one of those weekend-away seminars. They clicked, it seems, during a workshop for remedial teachers on a wet November Saturday in Salthill.

I can't help visualising her having awkward sex in a cheap seaside B&B, with him down to his Marks & Sparks Y-fronts, his leather-patched tweed jacket hanging on the quivering bed post.

But it must have been very different, because he's still very much around. I'm the one sleeping in a borrowed bed. Alone.

Clare told me all this herself, waking me up in the middle of the night not long after New Year to do so, in the oddest of fashions. I'd rather now that she hadn't. That I had remained blissfully ignorant and that I was blissfully ignorant still.

She shook and shook me but it was her sobs that made me sit up and take notice.

'What is it? Are you all right?'

She didn't say anything, just wrapped herself around me, like a child frightened by a thunderstorm might its mother. She was ashen-faced, her short fair hair dampened flat to her brow and she looked at me in that vague, scary sort of way. Just like a younger Matt used to when he had one of his nightmares.

Then she said it, out of the blue.

'I've been having an affair.'

'What? What *are* you on about?'

I was irritated now, but properly awake at last. She withdrew her shivering body and slid to her own side of the bed, turning to face the window.

'I'm sorry,' she said, her voice trailing off, 'I shouldn't have told you . . . '

And then she went perfectly still, the way people only in the deepest of sleeps can.

I didn't wake her because of what else she might say. This was enough to be going on with. I just sat there, perched against the brass bedpost, trying to make sense of this most peculiar of confessions. But the more I thought, the less I understood.

When the alarm went off at seven for work, I was no wiser. Just exhausted. I could hear Matt taking the stairs two steps at a time but Clare remained a crumpled heap, not twitching as much as an eyebrow. I suspected she was waiting for me to go, so I did.

That evening, after a few hours of tense politeness that encouraged Matt to take to his bed early, Clare parked herself on the couch next to me with two glasses and a bottle of wine.

'I better explain,' she said in little more than a whisper and she did.

I just sat there, toying with my glass and occasionally taking a sip, just to keep my lips wet. I said nothing and planted my focus on the blank television screen in the corner.

I know I should have been livid, thrown a tantrum, smashed the glass against the wall or at least called her a slut. I think she might have expected it, even have been relieved by it. Instead, I listened out of a bizarre mixture of curiosity and voyeurism. I got all the whens and the wheres in living technicolour.

After she had delivered her confessional monologue, she uncurled herself from a cluster of cushion and said she was off to bed. She put her head back around the door to tell me that I might feel better knowing that it was over now anyway. She wasn't seeing Him any more. But it didn't make me feel better, because I got an inkling that, if it was over, it was not her doing.

The night before she had been crying for Him. Definitely Him. Not for us or Matt and certainly not for me.

She didn't have to cry for long. He was back in a month, maybe less. I could read the signs from now on and tease out even the flimsiest evidence for myself. A cinema ticket here; a Visa bill there. And then there was that sailing course in Kinsale. Of all places. The cheek.

Maybe not enough to hang her in the Old Bailey, but more than enough to convict in my specially convened, non-jury kangaroo court. Guilty as charged. Guilty as hell.

# 4

## (Cork)

'Are you staying up?

'For what?

'The big fight tonight, ya dork.'

'Course. Ali will crucify him. Frazier on the floor in four. A quid says so.'

'You already owe me a quid, Danny. Said you'd move on Clare Fitz by last weekend and you didn't.'

'I'm meeting her later . . . '

'Too late, Sunshine. Pay up.'

'Fuck off, Flynnie.'

I make a wild swipe at him with my history book but miss, lose my grip and it skids across the tiled floor at a rate of knots, before stopping just short of Dirty Harry's desk, lying on its spine, the pages flapping wildly. I couldn't do it again in a month of wet Sundays.

Shit. I'm meeting Clare at half-four. If this fucker gets thick over this I'll be here till five. Minimum.

'Ah, Mr Hayes and Mr Flynn. Who else could it possibly be? Now, whichever of you scholars owns the volume at my feet, please retrieve it and then remind the rest of the class what we've learned so far today.'

Flynnie is beaming at me. Smug bollox.

'It's mine, sir.'

'Ah, Daniel. Come on up here now and tell us all about . . . Now what was it we were talking about again? Remind me.'

'Bismarck,' whispers Murph from my other side. A reliable source of information, I decide to go with that and walk to the top of the class and pick up the book.

'*Bismarck* sir. The battleship and all that . . . '

The tittering that had ricocheted around the classroom as soon as my history book shimmied along the floor is now converted into helpless laughter.

Dirty Harry shakes his head and smiles the sort of smile you'd expect Dirty Harry to smile.

'Sadly not, O Great Brainless One. We were, in fact, discussing the Franco-Prussian War. Bismarck was a pivotal figure in that conflict. The ship was subsequently called after him. Are the mists lifting?'

'Ya.'

'Ya?'

'Yes sir'

'And you are aware, I take it, that you'll be sitting a history paper in the Most Important Exam of Your Life next summer?'

'Ya. Yes sir.'

'Well take it from me, you'll fail. You haven't once given me a reason to suspect otherwise. But I don't tolerate failures and habitual messers in my class. So you can get out. Get out!'

I draw back my hair from my face and shuffle back to my desk, giving a so-what shrug on the way.

'I said *go*, Hayes.'

'Just collecting my gear, sir.'

'I didn't say go home, you moron. Just stand outside.'

'But it's the last class, sir.'

Dirty Harry has gone a sort of purplish red – he does so about twice a term – and he's bearing down on me.

'Oh, oh,' says Jimmy, thrilled skinny.

Dirty Harry's big rural fists are clenched.

'Get. Out. Of. My. Class. *Now!*'

I grab my bag and squeeze and weave my way to the door, with Dirty Harry never much more than an arm's length away.

Wide-eyed and apparently delirious, he has really lost it now and the class is in uproar, but I manage to reach the door just ahead of him. I can hear Flynnie yahoohing above everyone else.

I leg it noisily down the corridor, echoing all that way, too afraid to look behind and too busy to take a breath. As I take a handbrake turn left to the main door, I can hear the muck-savage screaming after me.

'You're for it tomorrow, Hayes. *Do you read me, Sonny?*'

I read you okay, you demented Kerry bastard. But tomorrow's another day. First, I have a date with Clare. Well, a sort of date anyway. And I'm in plenty of time too, thanks to you. Early in fact.

The lads will be talking about that for a while. The Day Dirty Harry Lost It With Danny. For once, I was the leading actor and Flynnie in a mere supporting role. It's my fifteen minutes of fame, and I plan to soak it all up.

The euphoria pales a shade as I near Clare's alma mater. I haven't had the time to get edgy or uptight about this date but as her school comes into view, I'm aware of a slight fluttering in the pit of my stomach.

This isn't like me, but then this isn't like my normal dates either. I don't usually meet girls after school. I'm not the schoolbag-carrying type. But when I rang Clare for a date, as I promised myself I would, this was the best deal I could get.

'Well, I thought we might go to the pictures. If you like.'

'That would be super, Dan. Thing is I can't. Not this Sunday anyway. But we could meet after school. Some day next week, maybe?'

So that was that. Not exactly the brush-off, but hardly the prologue to the hottest relationship date since Bonnie and Clyde either.

I have had my moments. Moments only, mind, and usually on a Saturday night with drink doing the talking and my trousers doing the thinking. For the sake of my reputation and pride these engagements are always talked-up the next day. All the lads do that and it's an accepted ritual. I'm sure girls do it too, or something like it.

The pictures on a Sunday night, according to Jimmy, are nothing more than a reward for favours delivered in these feel-and-fumble marathons. That's what he says, anyway, and there isn't a movie on general release that he hasn't seen.

Judy Roche is the only girl I dated for any length of time and that was only for a month or so. Then she made her excuses and dumped me, although I told it differently to my mates. That's accepted practice too. I reckon Judy thought I was bit of a loser and she's now dating some spiv in his twenties who drives a secondhand sports car with a broken exhaust.

Mad Mona, whom I dated only once, is not someone I like to be reminded of. Especially in Jimmy's company. It's only a cue for an unmerciful slagging.

Mona's reputation had preceded her, but I stubbornly persisted in asking her out anyway, on the strength of the passion she showed towards me when I walked her all the way home to Turner's Cross early one frosty Sunday morning.

After we had slapped tongues around and about our mouths for an age, she led my icy hands up under her blouse to her breasts, then she got me to endlessly tweak her nipples between my forefinger and thumb while she made the sort of noises Latin soccer commentators do when someone scores a goal.

I naively assumed that I'd make spectacular progress on a proper date, but it was more of the same. All I got for my endeavours was cramp in my left hand. If anyone had seen us, and I hope to God nobody did, I expect they thought we were a pair of aliens having it off.

Standing in front of her school and leaning against that ancient oak that overshadows it, Clare didn't look like a tweaker. And she didn't look as I had remembered her from a week and a bit ago either.

I was compromised that night, of course, by the near poisonous levels of alcohol that I had given refuge to. The next morning my head felt so heavy that I thought it would break off at the neck if I lifted it, and my stomach was just lying there like a wounded racehorse waiting to be put down.

Around lunchtime, the old man came in wagging a folded *Sunday Press* right in my face. We had words. Rather, he had words. I had silences, one for each of his questions. Defeated, he dragged open the curtains, pushed open the window and stormed back out. But I got up soon after because the room was bloody freezing.

'Hiya,' she says, her face turning on a welcoming smile when she sees me.

The friends she had been chatting to melt away, one staying long enough to whisper something in Clare's ear. Titter. Titter. At my expense, presumably.

'Hi. Been waiting long?'

'No. You're early.'

'Got out from school early, as it happens.'

'Great.'

I drop my schoolbag to the grass, stick my hands in my grey flannels and we stand looking at each other. Either one of us delivers a passable ice-breaker in the next few seconds or this is going to be a disaster. I'm superstitious like that.

One of us does. Clare.

'So who did you bring to the pictures instead of me?' There's a twinkle in her eye now and it's only as she walks towards me that I remember how small she is. More tidy really.

'Ah well, that would be telling.'

She points down the road. 'Will we wander down for a coffee?

I nod. Don't take coffee normally but I'll drink it today and like it.

'I'll buy, if you tell me who she is. I need to know what competition I'm up against.'

She gives me a little nudge with her arm, looks up at me and, with her big brown eyes, pleads again. 'Go on.'

''Twas Goldie Hawn actually. She's always ringing and

pestering me to take her out, so I brought her to see *Shampoo* and guess what . . . '

'What?'

'She was in it. Had forgotten completely. Didn't even remember making it. Proper airhead.'

When she laughs there's a husky quality to it. It's a very sexy trait that in a girl, although rare and undervalued. I'm taking note.

'So you didn't go to the flicks at all?'

'No. Stayed home, stared at the four walls and pined for you.'

Liar. Called over to Jimmy's, listened to Zeppelin and played poker until his mother threw me out.

Clare knows I'm teasing but blushes anyway and pulls her school scarf across her neck to disguise the fact. I think we're going to like each other. Well, I know that I'm certainly going to like her. I already do.

We argue over who buys the coffees.

'But I insist,' she says, 'you did own up about your date with Goldie, after all.'

I'm more insistent but sigh a silent one when she decides not to have the chocolate eclair I offered, because I couldn't have paid for it.

'I risked my whole future for you today,' I say to her when we sit down.

I lob two lumps of brown sugar into my cup before telling her, in elaborate detail, about Bismarck and his boat and Dirty Harry and his bad turn.

More of those cute laughs. She even pretends to choke on her coffee, which I think is a nice touch. She splutters, pats her chest and laughs some more. Then goes deadly serious.

'You're in deep shit, Dan. You must be,' she says, leaning across the table to me. 'Had Jimmy Flynn anything to do with this?'

'He started it, of course,' I answer, honouring him with a level of credit that he doesn't deserve.

'Should have known he'd be in there somewhere. The two of you are thick as thieves.'

'Well Jimmy is thick. You're right. But I'm just a thief . . .'

It's a bad joke but I'm on a roll and she laughs anyway. I'd tell bad jokes like that all night if she delivered that husky response every time.

I walk her to her gate. She lives in a well-manicured avenue of sturdy detached houses decorated with ivy. The last time I was around here it was four o'clock on a Sunday morning with Jimmy and we both peed into the petrol tank of a silver Merc.

My justification at the time was that the fat cat who owned it didn't deserve to and Jimmy's simply was that he had to piss somewhere. One of these night's it's going to be the parish priest's letterbox. It's on the way home and all.

'Well?' she says, leaning on a pillar.

'Sorry?'

'Are you playing hard to get, or what?'

'Christ. Of course. The pictures. You're on for Sunday?

'Yup. Love to see *Shampoo*, actually. But as you and Goldie have already seen it . . . '

'No. Just for you, I'll go again. To be honest, Goldie couldn't keep her hands off me all night. Hardly got to see any of it. You know the way it is.'

'No. I don't.' She gives me a smile, a wicked little wink and then the quickest of kisses on the cheek before running off up the gravel path to the hall door.

Then she calls after me: 'Who's gonna win the big fight?'

'Ali. KO. Are you into boxing?'

'Ya. Dad used to box at college.'

Don't like the sound of that. Hope he doesn't own a silver Merc as well.


As soon as I turn the key in the hall door at home, I can sense trouble. I have a nose for it and it for me. I have only one arm out of my coat when my father starts in.

He has a folded paper in his fist again, the *Echo* this time, and he starts to wave and jab it at me. It amazes me how a man who reads so many newspapers can still manage to know so little about what's going on.

Unfortunately, tonight proves to be the exception to that rule, because he seems to know more about The Day Dirty Harry Lost It With Danny than Danny does.

'Brother Leonard rang. Told me all about your shameful performance in class today . . . '

I walk past him into the living-room and slump down into the settee and pretend to watch the news. The sound is off but I watch footage of some barney in Derry or Belfast anyway. Predictable that, just like the old man.

He's standing behind me now.

'I'm talking to you. Are you deaf and stupid! Turn that damn thing off. I said turnitoff!'

The *Echo* is beginning to fray at the edges already but he pokes me in the back with it anyway.

'Are you listening? Brother Leonard said it was last chance saloon for you, boy. And he meant it. Teachers won't put up with it.'

I open my mouth to make a half-hearted defence of the indefensible but he stops me with another wave of his disintegrating baton.

'Don't waste your lying breath. That headmaster of yours is a decent man; he's giving you a chance you don't deserve. All you have to do to dig yourself out of this hole is to write a letter of apology to your history teacher, what's his name . . .?'

'Dirt . . . Mr Scully.'

My mother is hovering now, emerging from her kitchen to rein in the da, without appearing to give succour to her sinner son. It's a delicate skill she's learned in a long marriage that has yielded three children, me being the youngest by a yawning distance.

She says her piece too about how Kevin and Sheila never gave them any bother, although they never got what I got; how it's high time I went to Mass; and how this lazing about till all hours on a Sunday would have to stop.

After his steaming and screaming, which I refuse to acknowledge anyway, my mother's softly delivered but equally emphatic homily is the one I hear. Of course, hearing and listening are two very different things.

Good cop; bad cop. They think it works every time.

I compose the start of my letter to Mr Scully:

*Dear Dirty Harry,*
*Me and the lads were only saying the other day what a great ride your wife is . . .*

Some other time, perhaps. I write what I'm told and even promise my mother that I'll get down to the books from here on in. I'll go to Mass the odd day too. The sixth Sunday of every month perhaps. And there'll be no more of those late nights either.

Then I stay up until four a.m. to catch the big fight and wonder if Clare is watching too.

# 5

## (DUBLIN)

Clare takes her time answering the door. I can see her blur moving to and fro behind the frosted glass as she shuttles from the breakfast room to the dining-room and back. This is just one of her silly little war games but I'm not going to start positioning the heavy artillery over a minor provocation like this. Least said soonest mended.

I ring again, this time keeping my finger on the bell a lot longer, the way Matt's friends do when they call round. If this doesn't work I'll use my own key. It was only out of a sense of courtesy that I rang the bloody bell in the first place.

'Have you locked yourself out?'

It's my prying prat of a next-door neighbour who has a nose for what's tragic in other's people's lives, in compensation for the dreariness of his own. His ever-twitching snout will have sniffed something amiss long before now and it would make his day if I leant against the fence and made good his suspicions.

'Too dreary a day to be hanging about in the cold. Come on in, Dan.'

Not likely, old son. I was only in there once before when

I had to endure a three-hour discourse on how divorce would eat away at the fabric of Irish society and why he'd never allow his teenage daughter out in the sort of clothes her friends wear. I got one can of warm yellow-pack beer for my troubles.

'No, no. Clare must have dozed off or something. She'll be there in a minute. Thanks anyway.'

He doesn't look convinced.

'You sure?'

'Yes indeed, thanks again, Sean.'

Now fuck off in home and get out of your wife's underwear before she comes back from the shops.

'Righto, Dan, take care.'

I'm about to put my own key in the keyhole when Clare opens up. She instantly turns her back and walks straight into the kitchen. No traditional hiya. Not even a grunt. I follow wordlessly, not offering any greeting of my own and deciding not to ask why it took her half the average lifespan to walk along twelve feet, six inches of hall carpet.

'No chance of a cuppa, I suppose,' I say, dripping the sort of sarcasm that always got her on the defensive, even when she used to like me. Before she had me down as a wife-beater.

She folds her arms, leans against the table and nods towards the kettle. Nothing new in that. I fill it, plug it in and look at her, as if for the first time.

'So?' she says, returning my stare.

'Is that a "so, how ya keeping?" or a "so, how long will this take?"'

She smiles. But her eyes don't join in. This is Clare proving that she can be sarcastic too.

'So, how *are* you, Daniel?

'So, so.'

Clever that, even if I say so myself, but she doesn't bite. Doesn't say anything at all. I decide to – and get right to the point.

'That business the other night – I never meant to shove you like that, Clare.'

'Don't, Dan.'

'What do you mean "don't?"'

'I mean I don't want to hear any of it. I don't want to listen to your reasons today; you didn't want to listen to mine on Tuesday. I'd much rather you collected your stuff and went.'

The veneer of calm is gone. Clare looks pale and drawn now, like somebody who got out of her sick bed a few days too early.

I surprise myself by walking over to her and placing a hand on each of her folded arms. She tenses, but doesn't move and doesn't look at me either. Instead, she chooses to stare out into the darkening garden, nibbling at her lower lip.

'If I pushed you – hurt you – I'm sorry. It was totally out of order and unforgivable. But this has been a nightmare and I must have lost it. I'm truly sorry. Really, I am.'

I can hear my voice begin to crack and I can see that it's only pride and stubbornness that's stopping her from weeping herself dry. Part of me wants to fold her into my arms and hug her better but I can't and she wouldn't let me if I tried.

A bigger part of me knows that it's too late for all of that. The death certificate was issued last Tuesday. Funeral arrangements later.

I walk away, make the tea and sit down in Matt's chair. Nothing is said for a time and we both examine a different corner of the room. I hum 'Norwegian Wood' softly to myself but I can't imagine why and so I stop.

Clare takes a very deliberate deep breath and stares at me hard, her arms folded tight to her chest now. She's in charge of herself again but when she speaks her words are barely audible.

'Look, we've blown it, Dan. You and me both. You walked out last Tuesday. Fine. But if you had been awake the last three years, rather than just the last few months when the sex stopped, you'd have seen this coming.'

She tries to look me in the eye but I'm not up to it.

'Simply put, Dan: where the fuck have you been? You let me down then and that's when I started walking. I thought you might call me back some time but you never did.'

Going through the entrails of our relationship in the hope of finding out when and why it turned rancid is not what I want to apply my mind to at the moment. Some other time perhaps. Say around 2010.

At the moment though, I'm sticking to the script where I'm down to play the aggrieved husband. It's all I'm good for.

'As it happens, Dan, I've met a man who didn't just want a grope three times a week and who puts aside a bit of time for me.'

I raise my hands in abject surrender, like Italian footballers do when they're caught doing the dirt by the referee.

'Fine. Enough.'

It obviously isn't.

'But you still don't grasp it, do you? It's little or nothing

41

to do with me screwing somebody else. I'd never had met that somebody if you had been paying attention.'

I get up and pour a cup. Not that I want it but any distraction will do.

'So I'm a total shit and you are totally blameless. Rogering some horny bastard behind my back is totally irrelevant. Well, you learn something every day.'

It's my best shot, but my heart isn't in it.

'The sex wasn't the thing, Dan. I was lonely. Really, really lonely. And Rory was kind and still is.' The tears are poised side-stage again.

'Do you love this Rory guy?'

'Sometimes.'

'Which means?'

'It means sometimes.'

'I see.'

'No you don't. But have a think about it some day when you have nothing better to do. Just for the record. Just for me.'

I nod. But my heart isn't in that either.

She has her coat on to go now, something to do with the hockey team. A match in Sandymount. Under lights.

'Pull out the door after you, Dan. Though not as hard as the last time.'

This might be a little joke, or just more sarcasm. Either way, I don't find out because she closes the door gently behind her, as if making sure she doesn't disturb someone sleeping. There's no goodbye, just like there was no hello.

The phone rings and startles me but I let the answering machine do what it's good at and start to gather up enough gear to do me a week or so. It's strange how a house that I've lived in all these years seems so alien and foreign to me now.

Everything looks familiar, everything feels strange. Very odd.

Curiosity tempts me to play back the machine. It could be for me anyway; only a handful know I've jumped ship. But it's not. Instead I hear a voice that I've never heard before, but which I recognise anyway.

'Only me. God, the traffic from your place yesterday was woeful. Dead late for school. The little bastards were roaring the place down by the time I got there. Are you around for a quick pint after that bloody hockey? Call me if you are. Otherwise, see ya tomorrow.'

Click.

Prick. The cheeky prick slept here – it must have been Thursday night. And where did he buy the accent? I erase the message – no fucky-fucky for you tonight, teacher, sir.

# 6

## (Cork)

Jimmy couldn't believe what he was hearing. Sitting on the school wall and wrapped in a woolly scarf and duffel coat, he slowly shook his head and tut-tutted a few times.

'Well, who would have believed it.'

Jimmy was addressing a small cluster of lads who played rugby together and have the collective intellectual wattage of a bicycle lamp. They were leaning, slouching and loitering with varying degrees of intent.

'Poor old Danny Boy here *can't* come to Dublin for the match, because Princess Clare has put her foot down . . .'

I concentrated on jabbing my toe at a little pool of January ice that was trapped in a crack in the pavement and did my level best to look nonchalant. But this was hurting. I'd seen Jimmy circle the wagons on victims like this many a time but this was the first time I was the outgunned cowboy.

'It's got fuck all to do with her,' I lied, nodding in the general direction of her school. 'It's the old man . . . '

There was a cry of derision, even from that red-headed freak of nature, Moss Barrett, whose sex life revolves around the agony aunt page of his mother's *Woman's Own*.

I turned on him because he was the point of least

resistance. He reddened even more than genetics intended when I fixed him with my stare. Next to Jimmy's, my stare is the best out and about.

'So how many birds did you have to fight off you before you got to go on this trip, Romeo?'

He's a big, fit guy, quite capable of reducing me to stewing steak in record time but he died on the spot instead. A thousand deaths, actually. I felt like a heel then.

Jimmy bounced off the wall and came smack up to my face.

'You're out of order, Danny.'

'So was he. So were you.'

But Jimmy's no fool. He wasn't going to fall out with his best mate in front of half the school. And Barrett was dispensable anyway.

'For Christ sake, Danny,' he pleaded. 'It's Lansdowne. Against Wales. Loads of booze on the bus. Maybe a bit of Dublin pussy. Come on man . . . '

'Look, I'll beg the da. But he's being a right cunt these days . . . '

Totally irrelevant and Jimmy knew it too.

'Ah, leave it,' he said picking up his schoolbag. 'See ya.' Then he stalked off to join the others who had wandered ahead.

With my name now being written in freshly-made mud, I headed off home for another night of torturous swotting. Trying to get a two-year Leaving-Cert course crammed into a few months of hard slog is a bit like trying to get a kind word from the old fella. Next to impossible.

Jimmy was right, of course. My not going to the match had nothing to do with some parental diktat. My fate in this matter was sealed a month or so before when Clare and I cuddled up together in the Mutton Lane Inn.

We'd been seeing each other once or twice a week ever since that first coffee a few months earlier and with my eighteenth birthday just past, the subject of her seventeenth in January came up.

'Know what I'd love to do, Daniel?'

'What?

'Just to head off for the day. You and me. By train or bus or bike. Somewhere. Anywhere.'

'In January? 'Twill be freezing.'

'Ah come on. Pretty please . . . '

'You're mad.'

'Ah, it's my birthday. For me?'

Sensing that I was wilting, she coaxed and cajoled, gave me a hug, and that was that.

I wasn't to know that Jimmy and the boys were magicking up a coach and tickets for the Welsh game. Or that the dates were head-to-head.

Sounds like one gigantic piss-up too. There's even talk of one of the lads smuggling a few bottles of Paddy on to the bus. I'll be amazed if any of them are capable of figuring out how the turnstiles work by the time they reach Lansdowne. Some of them would be hard pushed at the best of times.

Four months ago my name would have been the first on the list. I'd have had nothing but sneering contempt for anyone who pulled out because it was his bird's birthday. 'Give her one on Sunday instead,' I'd have told him. 'Nothing like it to cure a hangover.' Har, har.

Truth is I never really wanted to go the match. All along I wanted to spend the day with Clare, doing whatever it is she wanted to do. Her arms draped around me and mine around her. Sentimental old tosh by any stretch of the imagination and something I'll only admit to when alone in my bed and without allowing my lips to move.

Truth is too that I might be falling in love, although I don't really know what that means and I'm not even sure I believe in such a thing.

I can get a handle on lust easily enough. We're old mates and have been ever since the day I discovered that what I carried around in the front of my underpants was more than a piece of primitive plumbing.

But love? I don't know, except that I have a lot of the recognised symptoms, the worst of which is humming treacly romantic ballads to myself when I'm not listening. If I hadn't these symptoms, I'd be on my way to Dublin for the match now and could stake my life on Jimmy and me still being blood brothers.

Maybe the whole thing is just a crush, an infatuation, or maybe I'm just flattered by her enduring attentions. It could be that when we meet at the train station this bitter winter morning for our magical mystery tour I'll wonder what the hell I'm doing there and wish I was getting rat-arsed on a rugby bus instead.

But when she runs up to me and lands a long kiss on my numb lips, I know that it's not going to be that easy. I know that I'm putty in her hands.

I return her greeting in spades, wish her a happy birthday and take her by the hand into the warm station café where we'll make up our minds about where to go.

As we sit there supping tepid tea, I slip her a birthday present. For a moment I feel like we're playing the leads in that old classic *Brief Encounter*, which was set in a railway station like this and is my mother's favourite film. I can see everything in fading monochrome.

'It's gorgeous, Dan. Beautiful. You're a pet.'

I should hope so. It cost me an arm and two legs, or rather it cost my big brother, Kevin. Making tidy money with his own little business, he's always good for a non-repayable loan. He bankrolls my Saturday nights too. An all-round good sport, even if he is the apple of my father's good eye.

It's a thread-thin delicate little gold bracelet. Not very rock-'n'-roll but I was stumped and returned to the first jewellers to buy it having sniffed around a dozen or so others. It was the first time in my life I spent more than half an hour shopping for anything. That could be significant.

She beams and wriggles her skinny wrist in front of me, leans across and gives me a kiss. I wish I could remember an appropriate line from the movie but I can't. It hasn't been on the telly for yonks. Instead, I tell her that the bracelet has to be back in the pawnshop by six, so we'd better get cracking.

'Where will we go?'

'There's a train to Cobh in twenty minutes.'

'Hardly the most romantic place on the planet, Dan, now is it?'

'No, but I know a lovely, cosy little pub with a snug where they do hot whiskeys that warm you to the big toe.'

Clare has never had a whiskey before, hot or otherwise. She guiltily makes this admission after her third and wonders can she have something else next time.

'It's the bloody cloves,' she says, edging one along her lips with her tongue until she can politely place it in the ashtray where seven others have been laid out in a neat circle.

The snug is as I remember it from that afternoon years ago, when I was brought here by my father who was treating an ancient grand-uncle to a day out. The old timer was frail and walked with the assistance of an ornate walking stick but he didn't need any help when it came to downing hot Jamesons.

I sat engrossed that day, sipping 7-Up as he pointed out through the snug window at the wide expanse of Cork Harbour, reliving his young life and reaching back to times that I thought could only be touched by history books. It was one of those days that stays with you, although you can't really be sure why.

The sun is sloping off now and its dying tangerine rays are reflecting off the choppy tide. A small tug is busy dispatching shift workers to and from the steel mill. It's about as pretty a picture as you're likely to witness.

'God, isn't it beautiful, Dan?'

It is, but I say nothing. We've been talking all day and I'm feeling comfortable and lazy now, so I give her a little squeeze instead.

In the far corner of the pub a mounted television is analysing the big match but I deliberately ignore it. The only indication I get of the result is when a loud voice, emotional on drink, declares that Ireland will never win anything if we keep on picking Dublin doctors and barristers.

'What we fucking need is more Cork blood-'n'-bandages,' its owner declares before letting himself out into the new night.

'It looks like Ireland got stuffed,' says Clare, giving me a nudge that suggests she expects a response this time.

'Probably. Typical Cork reaction too. Blame Dublin for everything that's wrong with the country now and blame the Brits for everything that was wrong in the past.'

'That's Cork for you.'

'Yep. And the reason I can't wait to get out of it.'

'Really?

'Honest. Dublin, London. Anywhere, just away.'

She's surprised at the determination in my voice and she turns to see if my face mirrors it. I'm even a bit surprised myself. I've never given this proposition a moment's thought before in my life and wonder where it came from. But now that I have said it, I'm fairly certain I mean it, although not for those reasons.

If I do uproot after the Leaving Cert it will have little or nothing to do with what's wrong with my home town. Being reared in a cardboard cut-out suburb in Cork city must be like being reared in one anywhere else. It's probably more to do with the old man. He might like me better from a distance and me him. Best thing really, now that I've begun to think about it.

Clare's all ears, sitting up straight her hands tucked palm-down under her thighs. We'd been chatting all day as we strolled up the steep hills at the back of the town and down Deep Water Quay but she's smart enough to know the difference between idle chat and real talk.

'Go on.'

'What?'

'So what do you want to do when you get to wherever it is you want to go?'

'Dunno'

'Jesus, Dan . . . '

'It's true, I don't. I'll think of something and I'll think of somewhere.' I don't know where that came from either.

Clare's looking at me really hard now and is thinking about saying something, but can't decide.

'Say it, whatever it is.'

So she does, in a hesitant way.

'Well, it's just that you're a hard one to figure out, Dan. You act the lunatic when you're with Jimmy Flynn and the boys. Nuttiest nutter on the block. Then when we go out, you're kinda deep. And the perfect gentleman.'

Me? Gentleman? I'm embarrassed so I laugh, a dead giveaway.

'And you get yourself thrown out of school and act the dunce, when it's obvious you have brains to burn. I'm lost.'

I don't know what to say, so I light up and try to make a pyramid of the beer mats on the table instead. The lads do it all the time; first to tumble buys the pints.

Annoyed with me for the first time, Clare waves away the smoke and wanders off to the ladies. By the time she returns, there's the making of a smile back on her face, a hot whiskey in one hand and a glass of lager in the other.

We say nothing for a while, then she kisses me on the lips. Not the sort of kiss we've been swapping all day but a kiss with some real heat in it. What they call smouldering passion in the books my mum reads.

'There's no need for you to answer anyway, Dan. I know all the answers.'

'So why did you ask?'

'To see if you knew them yourself.'

I sip my whiskey and she asks me do I want to hear them. I shrug, down the rest in one gulp, shudder and decide I'll have a Carling next.

She takes that to be a yes.

'Well, I don't think you're a nutcase at all, but you have to let on you are because that's what impresses Jimmy.'

'Bollox.'

'And you don't work in school because you wouldn't dare do better than Jimmy and the other slackers.'

'Brilliant, doctor. How much do I owe you?'

I'm enjoying myself, flattered that she sat down somewhere to work out this nonsense. She must be doing the same correspondence course as the old man.

'Finally,' she says ignoring me and rushing this bit, 'I'm beginning to think you don't really fancy me. Not deep down.'

Clare sips her lager and pretends to watch something on the faraway telly, satisfied that she's finally said what she's wanted to say all day.

It's hard trying to keep up with this girl. Take most girls out on a date and you're lucky to push the conversation beyond the height of Noddy Holder's platforms. This one obviously has a mind of her own and she doesn't tuck it safely under the pillow when she's going on a date either.

Not fancying her is not the problem. Fancying her too much is. It's one thing to try and undo some dizzy Deirdre's bra behind the stand, quite another to overstep the mark with the girl of your dreams and consequently blow it.

Dizzy Deirdre can tell you to keep your sweaty paws to yourself and you just go and find another Deirdre. But there aren't too many Clares around. I'm just being cagey.

I slide across the window seat to her and give her a hug and she puts those puppy dog eyes of hers on me.

'Well, do you fancy me, Dan?'

'Too much,' I say after a while, being more honest than I intend. I seem to be saying a lot of things today that I never gave the stamp of approval in advance. It must be the effect she has on me. Or maybe it's all those cloves.

'I fancy you too much too,' she says, running her hand up and down my thigh. We kiss again and I let my hand dwell on her sweater, close to her breast, the thumb tracing light little circles, tantalisingly close to her nipple.

'None of that now, if you don't mind,' the barman says, turning his head around the snug door to collect any empties. Startled, we untangle, and our hurried apologies fall over each other as they follow the poor mortified man out the door.

Then we collapse in laughter, she in that husky way of hers, like ten-year-olds caught with their hands in the biscuit tin.

Clare blames her shoes for tripping twice on the way down the hill to the station. Applying the sort of logic that is common currency at closing time on Saturday nights, she tells me that if she hadn't been drinking she'd trip much more.

We share sausages and salty chips out of a brown bag as we wait in the draughty, empty station for the last train home and she tells me that she'll be babysitting her twin sisters next Saturday night. Her folks are going to the Opera House, she says, and will probably head off for a drink with friends afterwards.

'I'll be there,' I say before she has the chance to make the invitation formal. I start the countdown there and then.

Maybe I should be concerned about how she's in charge of this relationship and seems to be reeling me in – slow, fast, slow – while I'm little more than an accomplice. A bit like she says it is between Jimmy and me. But today was too much fun for me to mull over maybes like that. I'm even willing to acknowledge that this love business is for real.

There's no reason in the world why Clare should know how I feel just yet. Just so she's doesn't think that she owns me. Not 100 per cent anyway. It makes things fairer.

# 7

## (DUBLIN)

I'm learning to hate the phone. Every time I pick one up I seem to be wrestling for the right word and phrase in an endless battle of wits with Clare. It's so bloody exhausting. And depressing.

We had words again the other night when I rang from work over what we should tell Matt about this sorry situation we've talked and walked ourselves into.

Clare wanted the three of us to sit down somewhere – she suggested Eddie Rockets because it's the little man's favourite – and tell him what's what.

'But Clare we don't even know what's what ourselves yet. At least, I don't.'

'Well I do.'

'Do you really? So Rory is it, is he?'

'Definitely maybe. Anyway, that's not the point. We've been through this already . . . '

I interrupted, my radar having identified one of her heat-seeking missiles coming my way.

'This person shouldn't be sleeping over, Clare. You know that. It's not right with Matt there.'

'Rory hasn't slept over, Dan.'

'He has, Clare. I heard one of his phone messages.'

'Only the once and Matt was in Cork. What do you take me for?' There was an edge to her voice.

It was late-night opening at the bank and Canavan was giving me one of those peculiar looks of his over his half-glasses. If this creep didn't exist, Dickens would have to be exhumed to invent him.

'Look. I'm busy. Really. We'll definitely have to sit down and talk soon. I'll pick up Matt on Sunday morning, elevenish, as arranged. Tell him if it's nice we'll hike, if not we'll go to the movies or something. All right?

'Fine. Bye.'


I could take consolation, I suppose, from the fact that we can be polite to each other now, if only just. Still, nothing is getting sorted. In fact, things keep getting unsorted. While I'm living out of a bin-liner in someone else's flat, my life is going on six miles away, without me.

Feeling sorry for myself is a hobby that I've devoted a lot of time and energy to but I know that it could be fatal at a time like this. Especially on the Friday night that I plan ringing my mother to explain what her Daniel has gone and broken now.

She'd be horrified if she knew the half of it, so I planned to tell her a quarter. It would be more than enough for a widow in her mid-seventies. And so it proved.

'Oh, son, that's terrible news. Terrible.' The Cork accent is always at its best when it carries a trace of misery. Practice makes perfect.

'Look. Don't worry yourself, Mum. It's not anything permanent or anything. Just, you know, one of those things.'

'I don't know, Dan, actually. My generation didn't have much choice. We had to stick it out. But I'm sure you don't want a sermon from me . . . '

I didn't and was grateful that she wasn't going to deliver one.

'I suppose I shouldn't ask what happened. Was it another woman?'

'No, Mum. No. Nothing like that at all.' I didn't elaborate. I had told her a quarter of it by now.

'And Matthew, the little pet? How's he? Poor darling.'

'He's grand, no bother. Honestly. Don't worry. In fact, he was in Cork with his other granny for a few days . . . '

She wasn't listening now and was invoking the ghost of my departed dad.

'I hope your father isn't looking down on this mess, Dan. Kevin and Sheila never gave your dad and me any trouble ever, you know . . . '

Her voice had a tremble in it. I was upsetting her. Mum knows me better than I know myself. As well she might. She has, after all, lit enough candles for me down the years to floodlight Wembley.

One memory seeps into my head, like a deadly odourless gas. It's of a particularly vicious row with the old fella, not a month before he died and not too long after I had left school. He turned to my mother, pointed a quivering finger in my direction and told her that two out of three wasn't bad.

'We can be rightly proud of Kevin and Sheila but this little shit isn't worth tuppence.'

My father never used language like that. Pillar of the Church and so on. Damn was as bad as it got. For him to bring that sort of language into his home and to use it in front of his wife was a measure of the man's contempt for me.

I found it hard to forgive him for that. Even on the day they lowered him into the ground I could feel the resentment swell up in me, standing in line with all those other emotions, the ones I was entitled to feel.

'Look, Mum, there's someone at the door, I've got to go,' I lied. Then I hung up.

My breath came in sharp little spasms and I went out on to the little balcony to gulp the night air. I gripped the banister so tight that my knuckles went white as I tried to wrest back control from the demons the phone call had unleashed.

I knew Peter, absent for the evening on a hot date, wouldn't mind if I raided his drinks cabinet. At that very moment I wasn't doing too well. In an hour I drank half a bottle of some nondescript Scotch and then went to my little room, switched off the light and sought out oblivion.

I slept like a baby. Exactly like a baby, in fact. Waking up every three hours. Crying.

On the morning after, my morose mood matched that of the weather perfectly. A sulky mist clung to the suburban rooftops all day, so I hid from it and everything else under a duvet until it was time for the football and rugby results. Peter was in his own room under his own duvet, but for very a different reason. The reason's name was Linda.

This morning things look different. The Sunday sun has the whole sky to itself and it's making the most of it. As I clip out the road to Shankill to collect Matt, I wish that it could coax me out from under my downer too.

Maybe if my numbers came up in last night's lottery. I hadn't checked yet. 7, 12, 16, 20, 24, 37. That might do it. Only might though.

Or a newsflash on 98FM, perhaps, about how the notorious Y-Front Man – aka Rory Bogtrotter – had been decapitated by a jack-knifing juggernaut. Splatter. That's a runner all right.

No such luck. Rory is very much alive. As I berth the Beetle in the drive, a car pulls up outside the gate and this bulky guy in a chunky sweater gets out. Our eyes meet for a fraction before we both look away. Not a bad-looking guy, I suppose, but whoever bought him that woolly thing on his back must like him even less than I do.

The front door opens before I reach it and Clare is standing there.

'You're late.' She virtually spits the words at me, possibly strung out at the prospect of having to introduce her husband and the father of her child to her bit of rural rough.

'He's early. Can't wait for it, can he.' I hope she can detect the sarcasm. As if she could miss it.

'Fuck you, Dan,' she whispers. 'Fuck. You.' We're back to basics now. Politeness is for normal people anyway.

Matt charges out of the house, throws his arms around me and then climbs into the Beetle, bellowing a greeting to Rory, who is standing self-consciously at the gate.

'Howya, Mattie my man.'

Mattie? There's a fucking limit.

Rory eventually summons up the bottle to come and stand by the rose bush where he fiddles with his car keys, faking composure.

Clare gives him a brave-little-soldier smile and taps me on the shoulder.

'Dan, Rory. Rory, Dan.' We've created enough electricity between the three of us by now for our own private thunderstorm.

He grins like an idiot but maybe I'm biased. Then he says hello.

'His name is Matthew or Matt,' I say, deliberating over every word and pointing to my son waiting in the Beetle. 'It might be Mattie in Ballysheepshag, but not where we're from.'

'Excuse me?'

'Ignore him.'

Her eyes blazing, Clare brushes me aside and ushers Rory inside as she might a pet labrador after its walkies. The house shudders as the front door thunders shut.

Don't think I made any friends there. But at least I might have spoiled their cosy day together. After that, nothing could spoil mine. I'm happy now. Not happy-happy, just fucked-up happy. But it will do.

# 8

# (CORK)

Clare turns out the lights and then hops back on to the couch, tucking her bare feet in underneath her, yoga style. We're completely in the dark. 'Let the show begin . . . '

I flick on the cigarette lighter I'm holding below my chin and floodlight my face as the eerie opening bars of 'Diamond Dogs' seep into every crevice of the room.

Then as Bowie begins the opening monologue, I mime his words with flawless precision. I've practised this a hundred times in front of the mirror at home, the sleeve-notes balanced on the mantelpiece as a prop. I've got it down pat.

Clare, with a generous sampling of her father's best gin sloshing about inside her, giggles uncontrollably. I'm bloody good at this, even better than I thought I'd be. There's nothing to this rock 'n' roll lark really. Like falling off a bar stool.

She has me giggling now. But I struggle on for the remaining half-minute or so and manage to get myself back into character for the end. The lighter flickers as I deliver the climax with a little extra flourish and then blinks once more before dying with the sort of dramatic finality that suggests that this might be my night.

I acknowledge the applause, dive on the couch and let Bowie get on with it. He's doing 'Rebel, Rebel' now and he doesn't seem to miss me at all. There's gratitude.

'Put on the light. I can't see a thing,' she says, trying to find me.

I reluctantly get up and switch on a discreet little lamp in the corner. It throws out enough light for us to see how much fun we're having but not enough to spoil the atmosphere.

'Are the terrible twins locked up in the attic for the night?'

'Next best thing. I've given them loads of Coke, a packet of Chocolate Goldgrain and I even allowed them to mess about with my clothes, on condition they don't dare come down and annoy us. They'll be good.'

Clare gets up and goes into the next room to see what drink we can experiment with next. She's careful not to take too much from any one bottle, so gin is off the list now.

'How about some Bourbon?' She sounds unsure. 'It's from when my uncle from the States stayed.'

'I'll try anything once.'

It's an impressive house. Everything is tasteful, nothing flash. There's a tang of tobacco in the air too. Her father must put his feet up at night with a cigar or possibly a pipe.

'Has your Dad his own practice?'

'Yep. Only a little one. Here, I put white lemonade in it. That's how Uncle Tim takes his anyway.'

It's revolting. Sweet and treacly but I swallow it. Waste not, want not.

'And why don't you want to do Law? You're smart enough.'

'Told you. I want to teach. Primary kids, not big oafs like you who walk out of school just to be on time for a date.'

'Aren't you glad I did now?'

She flops down on the couch and punches three enormous patterned cushions into exactly the shape she wants.

'I suppose I am.'

I put down my glass and join her and we talk and giggle and tell each other how wonderful we are.

Then we begin to kiss, lightly and playfully at first, but with more intent and inventiveness with every passing minute and they pass without us counting.

Bowie has stopped singing as if realising that three is a crowd, but neither of us has noticed. The kissing is provocative and aggressive now and our bodies are speaking the same language, although they're so close they only have to whisper. We're looking good, Houston.

Clare eases her hands inside my shirt and tracks her fingers up and down my back. I run my hand along her side and down her leg until it reaches the hem of her long skirt and then draw it back up, inside her clothes this time. Her thigh is warm and smooth and she smells of bubble bath and some faintly spicy scent.

My hand travels further and Clare stops kissing to undo her blouse. She doesn't bother to open the last few buttons and drags it over her head instead.

'Jesus, Dan, we'd better be careful. I don't know about this,' she says, doing one thing and pleading the other.

'We will. I will . . . '

She unclips her bra and takes in my expression as her breasts fall out. She smiles nervously, lets the straps slide down her arms and lies back. If I believed in God I'd be thanking him right now. And I thank him anyway, just in case. I shift my weight on top of her and she starts to tug impatiently at the belt of my trousers.

'We can't do the whole thing, Dan. You know that. It's too dangerous.'

There's an edge to her voice, as if she desperately wants to cry halt while she still can. I hear what she's saying, but the only thing that will convince me to put the brakes on at this stage is the word 'no'. And it will have to be shouted in capitals. This is as good as my life has got so far and appeals for caution are helpless in the face of it.

Then fate, the interfering bugger that she is, takes a hand. It doesn't register with me at first. It's only when the door bounces back off a door-stop and vibrates violently that the awful reality dawns. I frantically buckle up and fourteen pitiful excuses jostle for position on the tip of my tongue. Clare just freezes.

Two identical eleven-year-olds – wearing lipstick as war-paint, makeshift red Indian head-dresses and what appears to be the best of their big sister's clothes – come rampaging in.

After circling the couch quickly in fits of giggles and whooping like squaws on a girls' night out, they gallop back out the door. As their voices trail away up the stairs we can hear them chanting 'we could see Clare's titties, we could see Clare's titties . . . '

Clare is lying transfixed on the couch, unwrapped except for her panties and hoisted skirt, which lies crumpled around her midriff. She has her hands clasped tightly to her face.

'Oh fuck, fuck and fuck again.'

It's the first, second and third time I've heard her use

that word. It doesn't suit her at all.

When she takes her hands down, I half expect her to burst out laughing. But the Clare who climbs out of the couch, snatching her clothes from wherever they lie, is not in the humour for a comic turn. She's just angry. Angry as a rhino with a wasp stuck up its arse.

I get it first.

'You'd better go.'

What? What have I done?' I feel ridiculous now and hastily collect my scattered belongings.

'Just go, will you please.'

I dress slowly, out of spite. This isn't fair.

'Look Dan, I've got to clean this place up and then crucify those two poisonous little bitches upstairs.'

'Relax.' I look at my watch. 'It's barely ten.'

I put my arms around her waist and pull her towards me, but she's having none of it.

'No. Dan. They've wrecked it. Anyway, we were getting ahead of ourselves tonight. Stupid going that far . . . '

'Two minutes ago you were yanking at my trousers.'

'Well, maybe I shouldn't have. Not that there was any stopping you anyway.'

I don't like the turn this conversation is taking, so I throw my arms up in despair, give an exaggerated sigh, and toss various cushions looking for my jacket.

'You can hold on to the Bowie album until next week.' That's big of me in the circumstances.

'Take it, Dan. I don't like him much anyway.'

'Earlier you said he was great.'

'I was being nice.'

'Well, you got over being nice quick enough.'

'Dan, what if I got pregnant, for Christ sake?'

'Come on!'

'I'm not blaming you. I got carried away too. It was daft.'

'It's not as if you haven't done this sort of thing before.'

The words are barely in circulation when the alarm bells in my head start making a shrill noise.

'What did you say?'

Her hands are holding clumps of her hastily reclaimed blouse across her breasts. I can see that her nipples are still hard underneath.

'Nothing.'

'No. What do you mean by "as if you haven't done this sort of thing before"?'

I completely blank.

'Oh, I see. You reckoned I was a sure thing. So who was it?'

'Who was what?'

I can feel the heat on my face.

'Who said I was mad for it?'

'You're paranoid. Nobody. I'm off. Ring me when you calm down.'

'You don't need to answer, anyway. It was that reptile Keane. Steve Keane. I went out with him once. He spent the night trying to paw me and stick his tongue down my throat. I told him to get lost and he's told anyone who'd listen that he did it with me. Creep.'

She could tell from my face that she had more or less got it right. I could see from hers that she was going to burst into tears the minute I left.

'Oh shit, I'm sorry, Clare. Little runt. '

'So it was that bastard.'

'I've never spoken to the guy in my life, honestly.'

'No, but you ask Jimmy Flynn permission every time you take a leak and Jimmy and Keane play rugby together.'

I say nothing, which she correctly reads as a confession.

'Look, take your album and go. Tonight was a mistake. It's all been a mistake.' Very melodramatic but I think she means it.

I carefully slip the record into its sleeve and walk out the door.

'You're wrong, Clare, if you think that's why I asked you out. It isn't, honestly.'

I'm telling the truth now and I hope Clare can tell the difference. But all she says is goodnight and clicks the door closed.

I stand there for a while in the dark wondering what the hell has happened. One minute it looked like all my favourite dreams were coming true at once and in the same place. The next I'm being labelled a slimeball with a dodgy taste in rock music.

As I reach the gate I think I can hear identical screams coming from a bedroom. Hammer Horror stuff. I expect Clare's beating the twins to death with their jolly hockey sticks. I hope so anyway.


I make the mistake of walking into the sitting-room when I get home, forgetting how early it is. I often nip in there for a fag after a skinful on a Saturday night, sticking on the headphones and listening to a bit of Lou Reed. Lou's just the man for that time of night.

But the folks are there tonight. The da, thankfully, is snoring gently and my Mum has her head buried in a great slab of a library book. The telly is on with the sound turned down.

'What has you home so early?' Mum pushes her glasses down the bridge of her nose and looks at me inquisitively.

'I want to get a bit of studying in tomorrow and I don't want to be too knackered.' It shocks me how telling lies to both of them comes so naturally.

She smiles, asks me if I would like a bite of supper and places a bookmark on the appropriate page, as if anticipating my answer. But I surprise her for the second time tonight.

'No, I'm fine. Thanks.' Horslips are on the *Late Late Show* and I try to guess what number they're doing on our mute television.

She returns to her book, which has one of those period dust-jackets that historical romances look undressed without. This one has a beautiful redhead draped in a shawl gazing out over a headland, while in the background there's a handsome stud on horseback. They both look as miserable as I feel and I wonder if Clare is feeling miserable too.

But I can't allow myself to dwell on her now. I'd not sleep a wink. In the morning things might be clearer, although probably not. I wouldn't mind dreaming of her, though. I can still smell her and when I close my eyes, my fingertips can feel their way right up her silk-smooth thigh.

As I get up to go to bed, Mum places the book on her lap and asks me what time I want to be called.

'Called. For what?'

'Ah, Dan. Remember? It's your gran's anniversary and you said you'd come along to her Mass with Dad and me. Sheila and Kevin hope to make it too. It's not until half-eleven.'

I remember now, all right. A rash promise I made on The Day Dirty Harry Lost It With Danny. That was months ago.

'Right. Of course. Call me around elevenish so.' Shite.

She beams, obviously delighted that I'm actually keeping a promise. Maybe I won't turn out so bad after all.

At least one of the women in my life is happy tonight.

# 9

## (Dublin)

Matt folds and refolds the red paper napkin.

'That's typical of Mum. Always late for everything and I'm starving.'

True for him, but I'm in no hurry. I know from the phone call I made to arrange this family summit that Clare will not be in the mood for social niceties, even for Matt's sake. That's down to that little scene I created in Shankill last Sunday.

As I trampled the Wicklow hills later that day I almost summoned up the decency to feel sorry for Rory. But I kept that in check by reminding myself that he was probably snoring in my bed that very minute after a traditional lunch of roast lamb and mint sauce, followed by something tangy for dessert. Like Clare, for instance.

Ironic, I thought, how the only time they can have a poke these days is when I take Matt off somewhere for a few hours. I should turn back one day; tell Matt to stay in the car and stroll in unannounced. Just to see their faces, or whatever part of their anatomies they happen to be using at the time.

I tried hard on Sunday at giving Matt a good time.

Contrary to my worst fears, he didn't seem like a lad going through a crisis over his parents splitting up but that's probably only because the consequences of it hadn't dawned on him yet.

From what I could cull from an afternoon of snatched conversations on the subject, Matt saw Rory as a friend of his Mum's who was helping out because his Dad had left for a while. This must have been the line that Clare was selling the ten-year-old innocent when she was tucking him in at night.

But as we sit in Eddie Rockets now, I can sense that things have changed. Something isn't right, so I put out a few feelers.

'Did you have a good week, Matt?

'Yep'

'How did the football training go?'

'Grand.'

'Are you on the team for Saturday?'

'Dunno.'

These are the sort of answers Matt gives when he's in a sulk, or when there's something bothering him. Normally you can't shut him up. On long car journeys, like our annual trek to West Cork, we often bet him twenty pence that he can't keep silent for three minutes at a time. He's never once collected.

'Are you okay?'

He ignores the question and abruptly asks one of his own.

'When are you coming back, Dad?'

'Well, that's the sort of thing we're here to chat about today, Matt.' I look at my watch and wonder where Clare could be.

'It's just that, well I heard Mum and Rory talking the other night. I was doing my homework lying on the floor, the way I'm not allowed to, and they were on the couch. They mustn't have seen me or something. I didn't mean to listen . . . '

I'm intrigued and encourage him to continue, while trying to appear indifferent.

'Mum would be mad if she knew I was talking about this.'

'It will be our secret.' I say, lowering my head to his level and looking him straight in the eye. I'm not sure of my motives on this one just yet but it's even money that they're not all honourable.

A cute and cheerful young Spanish waitress comes to our table and asks do we want to order now. It seems senseless to wait any longer. Matt orders his usual but his heart isn't in it. I ask for a tuna melt and a mug of coffee.

'Well, I think that Rory wants to be my new dad or something,' he says after she goes, unsure of himself and looking at me intently so as to gauge my reaction.

'Don't be silly. How could he?'

'Cause you left on Mum and now she wants Rory.' He's getting upset and he sniffles hard and wipes his reddening eyes with the end of his sleeve.

'Tell me. What did they actually say, Matt?' I speak softly, but the urgency in my voice slips through. He seems eager to unload the information anyway, probably hoping that sharing the burden might lessen it.

'Rory was saying that Mum was the first woman he ever wanted to have children with and Mum was saying to be patient and wait and see.'

He's blubbering now, but he gathers himself together and continues, the words tumbling out as fast as his confused mind can manufacture them.

'But I don't want a stupid baby brother or sister now and I don't want him as my dad. I thought he was Mum's friend, but he wants to be her husband and she'll divorce you and you'll go away . . . '

I place my hand on his arm but he shakes it off impatiently and refuses to be mollified.

'Why can't things be like they were before that stupid fight? Why did you have to go around the house shouting at Mum and making her scared? You didn't even say goodbye to me.'

'I'm so sorry all that happened, Matt. Honestly.' My own heart is pounding now.

'But why don't you say sorry to Mum? You're always telling me not to lose my temper and to be sorry when I do . . . '

'I have, Matt. I have. Really.'

He's breathless and wordless all of a sudden and he picks up the napkin he was playing with earlier to wipe his eyes and noisily blow his nose. I can tell that he feels the better for it already but he goes to great lengths to avoid my eye.

A frumpy, middle-aged woman sitting at the counter, who had swivelled around to have a good nose, has switched from staring at Matt to glowering at me. I give her five seconds to start minding her own business before fixing her with a glare that would turn Hannibal Lecter into a bedwetter. Then I go round to the other side of the table and slip in beside Matt.

'Look, Matt. And I swear this to you. I'll always be your

dad. Your only dad. And I'll always be there when you need me. Understand?'

I sound like I'm auditioning for a bad part in a stinker of a mini-series but I can't think of any other way of saying what I know he desperately needs to believe.

He leans into me and shudders like he was caught in a sudden draught but he has no more to say.

'Ignore what you heard. It was only words. Mum probably didn't want to hurt the guy's feelings or something like that. Really, that's all it is. Or maybe you misheard. Try your best to forget it. Delete it from your memory.'

'Okay,' he says, but he needs convincing.

'You know the way you define and delete on the computer at home?'

'Yeah'

'Well, just like that.'

'Okay.' A small bit better.

'I can understand if you're angry with me, you know. But I'm trying to put things right now. Both of us are.'

'I'm not angry. Just a bit worried and stuff.'

He's worn out from it all and I decide to tell him the one bit of good news that I can think of to shake him out of himself.

'I bet you don't know where you and me are headed in the New Year?'

'Where?' He sits up now, sniffling. A bit of light comes into his wet eyes.

'Anfield!'

This was organised months ago and was supposed to be a surprise for his birthday but this seems like a better time than any to tell him.

'What? Really? Who are we playing?'

'The bad guys'

'Man U?'

'The very ones.'

'Yesss. Oh thanks, Dad.' He turns to give me a hug and then announces that he feels his appetite coming back.

'Run down to the loo, wash your face, blow your nose and by the time you get back your burger and chips will be here.'

He's hardly gone when the waitress comes and places our food on the table and tells me, in heavily accented English, to enjoy my meal. But it's a stiff drink I need after all that and I promise myself one as soon as I get out of here.

I close my eyes and press my hands flat against my face and drag them down from brow to chin. When I open them again Clare is sitting opposite me, eating one of her son's french fries and looking every bit as frazzled as her ex-husband.

'Oh, hello.'

'Hi.'

'Where have you been? We had to order.'

'Don't, Dan. I've spent the last two hours in casualty. Conor Quinn was messing in PE and somehow managed to split himself open. What a nightmare. When his stupid tramp of a mother came into the hospital the first thing she said was that she'd sue the school. Cow. Didn't cross her tiny mind to ask how her lunatic son was. She got no change out of me, I can tell you . . . '

'So how many stitches did she need?'

She ignores me, drags off her coat, balls it up and throws

it in the corner of the cubicle with unnecessary force, catching the sugar canister which topples and rolls along the table, spilling its load as it goes. The girl doesn't know her own strength. Never has.

'Shit.' Clare means to whisper it but it comes out as a half shout.

Noseybag at the counter thinks about throwing a quick glance over her shoulder but corrects herself in mid-turn. I burn a hole in her back with another stare and she shifts her wide, sagging arse uncomfortably on the stool. Imagine having that sitting on your face. Goodnight.

Clare lifts her fringe out of her eyes and asks where Matt is. She should get her hair cut, it suits her better short.

'In the loo.'

'I could do without this let's-talk-about-it session right now, to be honest. I'm wrecked.'

'Well, we've already had a chat. He's been a bit upset, asking when I was coming home and stuff. He's fine now, so don't make a fuss.'

'What did you say to him?' Her tone is bordering on the belligerent but I let it pass.

'I just tried to reassure him. Said that I'd always be there. You know, what could I say? Anyway, I wouldn't say any more to him today.'

She drops her head in her hands, rubs her eyes and looks at me.

'What a mess, Dan. Poor little fella . . . '

Before I can take the conversation further, Matt slides in next to me.

'Hi Mum.'

'Hiya pet.'

Clare can see that he's been crying and she looks at me but doesn't say anything.

'Guess what, Mum?'

'What love? You got twenty out of twenty in your spelling test?'

'No. Twelve actually, but don't mind that – guess where me and Dad are going in the New Year.'

'Where?' She sits up alert, her eyes bright with anticipation. 'He's not dragging you up the mucky mountains again, is he?'

'No, no. Liverpool. Anfield. For the United game . . . '

She knew all about this birthday treat and understood in an instant why I had told him now.

'Wow!'

'What's the exact date, Dad?'

'Can't remember, but it's the last Saturday in January. A long time away yet.'

'I don't mind, it's the looking forward to something that is the best part anyway.'

All three of us smile and then Matt turns his attention to his fries, burger and milkshake.

'I'm starving,' Clare says, eyeing my sandwich. 'Are you not eating that?'

I'm not so she devours it, asking the Spanish waitress for a mug of tea and some apple pie with cream.

I just sit there and watch the two of them eat and wonder why I'm not going home with them tonight.

I give Matt the money to run ahead and buy his *Match* magazine and Clare and I walk in silence towards their car. My car too, but what of it. I begin to say something just as

Clare does and our words collide, head on.

'No, you first,' I say. This politeness is unnerving but with Matt in his present confused state of mind any hint of tension between us would be irresponsible. Besides, neither of us has the fight in us tonight. Clare can't even muster up the energy to ambush me about last Sunday.

'You walked the legs off Matt up the mountains. He had a great time.'

'Ya. It was a pet day. But I expect you didn't see much of it.' I couldn't stop myself getting the barb in and regretted it straight away.

'Oh, Dan. I'm too tired. If you want to think that Rory and me spend every waking moment shagging ourselves silly, well that's your problem.'

'I just meant . . . '

'I know exactly what you meant, Dan. I always know what you mean even before you think it. Twenty-two years, remember?'

Matt is galloping down the footpath in our direction, leaping every few yards to head imaginary balls past imaginary goalkeepers. Goooal!

'Besides, Dan, whatever we got up to on Sunday afternoon couldn't have been as pitiful as your display with Rory on Sunday morning.'

One dig each seems fair, so we leave it at that. We can agree on that much at least.

A breathless Matt joins us and points up the road. 'Look who's coming.' It's Liam and Sally, friends of ours we haven't seen in months, their three children trailing behind. They're waving at us. Normally we'd be happy to see them, but not tonight and not in these circumstances. We wave back.

'Liam. Sally. Hi . . . '

Clare powers on the charm and I take my cue from her, getting a sort of pathetic comfort from the fact that we're still a team when it comes to some things. For another small while anyway.

The four of us talk across each other while their two younger kids race around the pavement playing chasing with Matt. Their eldest, a sulking teenager, hangs back listening to his Walkman, his shoulders dropped and his hands buried in his baggy jeans. Looks like a right surly handful. He reminds me of someone, but I'm not sure who.

'Look, you two have got to come over for a bite some Saturday night,' Sally says, 'I'll ring you next week Clare . . .'

That only took five minutes but I'm drained anyway. I think we both are. Neither of us had been sure if the other was going to say something. But neither of us did.

Silly really, but it's probably because every time you tell somebody that it's over, you take another brick out of the wall. Our marriage might be a derelict, condemned ruin at this stage but I still can't bring myself to publicly dismantle it. Perhaps Clare can't either.

After seeing Clare and Matt to their car, I head to the nearest decent pub and order that stiff one I had promised myself. Then I remember who that moody teenager reminds me of. Myself, of course. That gives me my first chuckle in ages.

# 10

## (Cork)

Father Sheehan clears his throat, not bothering to turn his mouth from the microphone. The magnified sound echoes to the church rafters and a few of the congregation can't help but shudder in disgust.

There is no apology forthcoming, he just dabs his mouth with a crumpled and matted hanky before fixing his flock with a long, baleful stare. He has our attention now all right; only the odd whimpering infant and the occasional muffled cough offer any competition.

'Last night, dear people,' he says, his mouth tucked up to the mike and his voice little more than a conspiratorial whisper, 'a caller came to my door. Someone unexpected. Someone unwelcome. Someone ungodly.'

He throws in a long pause here, just for dramatic effect. Sheehan knows how to work a crowd. This is rock 'n' roll for the rosary bead generation and I'm seriously impressed.

'Who was this caller, you might ask?' He's speaking a little louder now and his bald head and face have gone Che Guevara red, belatedly catching up with his nose, which has been that colour all along. A drinker's nose if ever I saw one. Good man.

'I'll tell you,' he says leaning over the pulpit like one of those American bible thumpers, 'I'll tell you.' Then he lets us wait again before roaring out the word, a word that still has a ring to it, even in the seventies.

'Satan!'

Sensing that his dear people, now shuffling in their seats, are taking him at something less than his word, he repeats himself, only louder this time. Much louder.

'*Satan!*'

I have visions of Fr Sheehan having a horizontal jog with his buxom housekeeper, only it isn't her at all but the devil himself in drag. I allow myself a quick smile and then catch my big brother's eye, which has a twinkle of its own in it.

The parish priest's story isn't that funny, though. It's much funnier.

'And do you know what Satan did when he called unannounced and uninvited?

Nobody did, so we wait to be told.

'He urinated. Yes, dear people, he ur-in-ated. Through my letterbox, using a bunch of young drunken yobbos to do his . . . his . . . dirty work.'

I nearly choke. Jimmy. The mad bastard. He did it. Said he would. He actually did it. I don't know where to look; all I know is that if I catch as much as a glimpse of this druid's florid face again this morning they'll have to operate to stop me laughing.

After last night's débâcle at Clare's place I didn't think I'd raise a smile for a long time. I put it all down to what my father would call the redemptive power of prayer, so maybe I really should go to Mass more often. Wild.

'What sort of people of people would do such a disgusting thing?' my mother asks my father as we drive home.

'God only knows,' he says shaking his head sadly, 'but horsewhipping's too good for them, whoever they are.'

Sitting in the back, I lift the *Sunday Press* in front of my face, because I know that any platitudes I might manufacture for the occasion couldn't possibly be corroborated by my face. I even try to change the subject.

'Charlie George got a hat-trick yesterday. Some player.'

My father gives a non-committal grunt and indicates right to go up our park.

I drag my bike out of the garden shed and I'm shocked at the state of it but it will have to do. Jimmy has arranged a soccer match on the green near his place and if I hurry I'll get a game. A few weeks ago he'd have phoned to tell me but we're not that buddy-buddy at the moment and I only found out because I rang him. I didn't dare mention the morning's panto, though. The walls in this house have cauliflower ears.

The squeaky wheels attracts my mother's attention. She's doing the dishes after the dinner and she peeps out the kitchen window as I hop up on the saddle.

'So much for you studying today,' she says, wagging a sudsy finger at me. She's keeping her voice down so that the old fella won't hear.

I point a thumb over my shoulder at the backer, which is stacked with four of the thickest schoolbooks I own.

'Me and Jimmy are going to get stuck into these this afternoon. I thought I mentioned it.'

She smiles and waves me off. I don't know if she believes

me or not. Sometimes I think she just pretends for the sake of peace and quiet. The last thing she wants on a Sunday afternoon is the da folding up the newspaper and waving it about the place before she's had a chance to read it.

I often wonder how she'll cope when he takes early retirement from Ford's next summer. It's not that early really, he's at least sixty-three and although he doesn't look it, I know he feels it.

I overheard him tell the mother once that the job had sapped all the life out of him and I felt a twinge of pity for him at the time. It can't be much fun being a wages clerk at seventeen and still being one in your sixties. I could never imagine anything like that happening to me. Different times and all that.

Jimmy makes a fist and punches the air in the midriff twice when I tell him about this morning's Mass.

'I should have been there, Dan. It must have been fucking wild. What exactly did the old bugger say?'

I take him, and a small cluster of apostles, through the whole performance from the snotty handkerchief to Sheehan's graphic description of the actual Satanic ritual itself.

Gerry Clifford goes pale and quiet all at once.

'Jesus. He didn't see anybody's face did he?'

'Were you there?'

'Cliffy was my lookout but he was so pissed he fell asleep against a telegraph pole.'

'Well, did he? Did he say he saw anyone?' Clifford is bordering on the frantic. No point going on this sort of mission if you haven't got the bottle for it.

'Doubt it. But he did say the cops are going to make

83

house-to-house inquiries . . . '

Clifford melts away with the football and starts whacking it against the boundary wall, trying his best not to look like a condemned man. I'd bet my last fifty pence that he'll have an early night next Saturday, probably taking his chemistry books to bed with him. Swot.

'You missed a cracker of a night, Dan. That's something like three in a row. Hope she's worth it.'

'Actually, Clare and me are history.'

'Oh. Since when?' Jimmy's all ears.

'Since last night. Decided to call to it quits.'

'Who did. You or her?'

'Me, I suppose. It was getting too complicated and time-consuming.'

He'll guess that I'm lying but nobody blubbers all over his best mates about how he was dumped. It would be bad for the collective ego. Jimmy wouldn't thank me either for telling him that his name was dragged through the mire by Clare and used in evidence against me.

'Well, your timing is perfect. There's a big party next Saturday and it's going to be something else. You on?'

'What do you think?'

It's good to be back. All I have to do now is fall out of love with Clare and I'll be right as rain.

We have enough players for a six-a-side, but I find that my revelation to Jimmy has sucked me back into a black hole, exactly where I was before the miraculous intervention of the One True Faith this morning.

When the first ball comes to me I put my foot on it and look around in the imperious manner of a Franz Beckenbauer, only for my feet to be swept from under me by a thundering sliding tackle. The ball remains aloof from the proceedings while I do an unrehearsed somersault and crash-land in the most awkward and undignified manner.

Looking down at me is Moss Barrett, extending a hand to help me up.

'Sorry about that,' the big red-head says, having done exactly what he had intended to do and looking pretty pleased about it. I had ridiculed him in front of his mates a couple of weeks ago. This was payback time.

'No sweat.' I grimace and accept his hand. We're quits now. Not a bad bloke really.

If there is anyone to blame for me ending up arse-sore and delicate it must be Clare. If I didn't have her on my mind I wouldn't have dwelt on the ball that crucial second too long and Barrett's vengeful lunge would have been wasted on the damp afternoon air.

From here on I try to concentrate on the football and I'm consoled by the fact there's one other participant with more on his mind than me. Poor Cliffy is running around aimlessly, with a look of impending doom on his long face. Any minute now he expects a crucifix-wielding Sheehan to lead a mob of torch-carrying parishioners right to us.

Unfortunately, that does not happen.

The last thing Jimmy says to me before I head for home dishevelled, sweaty and sore is to hang tough. He has twigged that my mind was absent without leave all afternoon and is afraid that I may be tempted to try mend fences with Clare.

I think he looks on my returning to the fold as a little personal triumph. Despite his reputation with the birds, which he has taken great care in cultivating, he's really a lad's lad. He'll probably turn out to be a man's man too, still pissing where he shouldn't when he's an old lad.

'Whatever you do, Hayes, don't phone her. I know how your mind works, you big soft gobshite.'

'Course I won't. It's not a problem. Like I said, history.'


The first thing I do when I get in the door is ring her.

Well, it seems like too good an opportunity to waste, seeing as both parents are out, presumably on one of their Sunday rambles down around Blackrock Castle and beyond. They'll be ages. We might even have time to iron this whole mess out.

As I dial, I'm hoping for two diametrically opposed things to happen. I'm desperately hoping Clare takes the call and I'm desperately hoping she doesn't.

I'm surprised when someone answers on the first tone and I'm even more surprised that it is her. Great. Shit.

'It's me.'

'Hiya.'

'Just rang to find out if the terrible twins are still alive.' Pathetic, but I'm making this up as I go along. It's like live TV.

'They're fine. Look, I can't really talk now.'

'Right. Well, can I ring back later, maybe?'

'No, not really.'

'Well, meet you after school tomorrow?'

'I can't.'

'Some other day then?' I'm getting desperate now.

'Fine. But next week is mad. Give me a ring.'

'I'm sorry about last night, Clare.' I'm not at all sure what I'm sorry about really but I'm sure she expects me to go through the motions anyway.

'I've got to go, Dan. I'm sure I'll see you around.'

See me around? Christ, she's giving me the brush-off. I go cold inside, but before I can contemplate some totally inadequate response, Clare throws a breezy 'see ya' down the line and gently replaces the receiver.

Click.

Jimmy was right. Sometimes I hate him when he's right and this is one of those times.

If I had any contacts in the CIA, I'd ask for transcripts of everything we said to each other last night. Maybe then I could get a handle on what really happened. All I have to look forward to now is some dodgy party next weekend and I'm not looking forward to that at all.

# 11

## (DUBLIN)

'Could you drop in, please.'

Mark Danaher's phone calls are like that, curt and not lumbered with any of the normal niceties. That's why he's a thirty-two-year-old manager who reckons he's barely started and I'm a thirty-nine-year-old assistant manager who knows he's finished.

When he has a few jars on him, which is most Friday nights, he tells those in his inner circle that he's only passing through and that he fully expects to be a regional manager by the time he's forty; a three-star general by the time he's forty-five and tending his own vines in the Loire Valley by the time he's fifty. Prize prick.

I don't belong to what he calls his team, which includes some of the young and acned, and of a few of my own vintage who like to pretend to their wives that they're still ascending the career ladder. In reality, all their brown-nosing could possibly achieve is a decent enough Christmas bonus to make a down payment on a leaky mobile home in Wexford. Hardly worth selling your soul for.

I used to tell Clare that if she ever saw me showing any of the behavioural habits of *Homo Arselickus* that she was to hit me hard over the head with a blunt instrument and then let me bleed until I twitched my last.

Just to watch this species operate in the pub on a night when Danaher is holding court is too much for me. The more obvious ones just elbow their way into his immediate circle and could only be displaced by water cannon. The more subtle hover at a respectable distance, feigning lack of interest, until an opportunity presents itself for them to slither in. Just the thought of it makes me shudder.

Sometimes I do feel that although I can't and couldn't play these degrading games, I should at least try to camouflage my contempt for them. That way Danaher wouldn't call me into his poky little office ever so often to slap me about the place.

I knock, enter and take a seat. He doesn't like that; he'd much rather I stood while he studies whatever it is he pretends to read when I walk in. Deputy Dog Dick Canavan is sitting in too, which means this is more than a routine dressing-down. I could do without this.

Danaher looks up, but doesn't bother with the mechanical smile this time. Instead, he shoves a sheaf of papers across his desk at me. If I didn't stop them they'd scatter all over the floor. He's in a stinker.

'How can you justify this?'

'Sorry?'

'That piece of fucking disgraceful underwriting that you've put your name to.'

My eyes race to the end of the last sheet and my name is there all right, but I can only vaguely recall approving this loan. And it's for ten grand too. Shit. Think man, think.

'What in the name of Christ were you thinking of ?'

89

'Has it gone bad, Mark?'

'Has it gone *bad*. Well, I didn't call you in here to present you with the Nobel Fucking Peace Prize, Dan.'

Canavan squirms in his seat or at least he pretends to. He'd like me to think that he finds the manager's methods distasteful and he'll probably confide as much to me later. But I know his type: banks breed them like hothouses do exotic plants and squirming as an indication of moral outrage is not something that comes naturally.

'I'll get on to it right away.'

It's all I can think of to say. I might not be the Messiah's gift to banking, but I do like to think of myself as an old pro and a bloody good lender. This one hurts, especially as it gives the spiv Danaher a chance to draw blood.

'I'll tell you this much, Dan. You'd better and damn bloody quick too. I'd expect more from one of my senior people. A lot more, quite frankly.'

One of his senior people? I'm not one of his anythings. But I let it pass, because I have no other choice and because I always do.

When I walk into the body of the bank I realise that I'm sweating and I notice that I'm attracting sympathetic and curious glances from colleagues. Obviously, the word was out that Danaher had Hayes by the privates this time. Thanks for the warning, one and all.

I hardly have my feet under my desk when Sinead Burke propels herself across the floor on her swivel chair. She's wearing that mother-hen frown of hers, which she keeps in her drawer for little office catastrophes like this one. It puts years on her.

'I meant to warn you. Canavan had me rooting out files

this morning. One of his little witch-hunts. He said the manager was like a bear with a sore head. If I can give you a dig out at all, just ask.'

'Thanks.' I try a smile and wish she'd go away.

'As if you haven't got enough troubling you at the moment.'

I thought I had been discreet about the break-up, no wailing into my pint or anything like that. Obviously not discreet enough. No more calls from the office from now on.

'Look, I'm not really going public on that one, Sinead.'

Realising that she has spoken out of turn, she nervously starts re-arranging her bra strap by pinching at it through the shoulder of her blouse. I've seen her do it so often when she's under pressure. Poor old Sinead, she means well. It's just that her loaded mouth can be as lethal as someone else's loaded Magnum.

'Oh God, me and that big gob of mine.' She throw her eyes up to heaven.

Tall, thirtyish, with long fair hair, Sinead is never short of a hormonal male or two drooling all over her. She wards off the pests by telling them about her prison-officer fiancé in Portlaoise and ensnares the more presentable by wearing skirts that end just below where they begin and tops that plunge as far as your average bungee jump.

It must be this enforced sex drought that has me sitting back and fancying a workmate who sits three yards away. And in the middle of a crisis too. But I allow myself thirty seconds to imagine what it would be like with Sinead. I can see the windows of the Beetle all fogged up and she astride me and putting enough effort into it to satisfy the whole

Irish pack. As if I would. As if she would.

Still, if I don't get my end away soon I'll end up like Canavan, all mean mouth and narrow eyes. And if I don't get to the bottom of this loan fiasco soon I'll end up stacking cheques in the basement of bank headquarters. I put Sinead to the back of my mind and file under Never Say Never.

I work through lunch, taking a BLT and warm Diet Coke at my desk. Not that I have any great expectation of getting the bank's money back, but I'm vaguely optimistic that I'll find out something that will muddy the waters sufficiently to make tomorrow's summons to the inner sanctum a little less degrading than today's. But I run up more cul-de-sacs than a blind man in a marathon.


Heading home late, I stop and grab a Chinese and wonder should I get something for Peter too but then decide against. Actually, I hope he's out, because I'm not in the humour for company tonight. There's gratitude for you.

But not only is Peter in but he's got female company and they're sitting at the seldom used dining table eating a very elaborate dinner that either he or she has spent a long time preparing.

Peter even has that awful Vivaldi tosh on at volume one and the lights are down. Romantic or what. Now I've walked in on them, carrying a brown bag that's about to leak black bean sauce everywhere.

'Ah, Dan.'

'Hi. Sorry to interrupt. I didn't know that you're were doing anything special.'

'I thought you said you were going to take in that new film by whatshisname?'

'Mike Leigh. Shit. So I did, Peter. I had a nightmare of a day and forgot all about it.'

'No sweat. Pull up a chair.' Then he introduces me to Linda.

She's been about a lot lately, a milestone in itself, considering Peter's chiselled-in-stone maxim about changing girlfriends as often as the Italians change governments.

How does he do it? I can't even get my wife to sleep with me. He's pushing forty and nobody will ever mistake him for Richard Gere. Still here he is.

Perhaps it's because he's a very fine human being with an innate sense of decency. Gorgeous women like Linda, who wear drop-dead sexy little numbers and boast low mileage on the clock, could well be suckers for the sort of thing.

Or maybe it could have something to do with the fact that he's a loadsamoney executive with one of the more prestigious merchant banks, which makes him a real banker and not a piggy-banker like me. Or even that he drives an orgasm-on-wheels motor.

Who knows. It would be wrong of me to draw any cynical conclusion after all he's done for me.

I give Linda my broadest smile and she gives me the class of greeting that she must normally reserve for drunks in bus queues or Saturday morning Jehovah's Witnesses. If she had rented three hundred billboards, I wouldn't have got the message any clearer. I'm intruding.

'Look, you two carry on. I'll pour this on to a plate in the kitchen before the bag disintegrates.'

'Ah join us, Dan.' He doesn't mean it although his voice nearly pulls it off. Linda concentrates on swirling red wine gently around her glass.

'No, thanks all the same. I'm knackered anyway. Nice to meet you, Linda.' Not.

She throws me a cast-off smile the way she might throw a meatless bone to a stray mongrel.

I can't get out of there quick enough, but I find that the kitchen, which is little more than a galley is littered with the debris of the meal they are now getting back to eating. I force open a corner of space at the edge of the counter and try to eat my dinner from the container while standing.

I was ravenous when I turned the key in the door, now I'm turning the food over in my mouth and wondering can I swallow it. I'd feel sorry for myself if I thought it would make me feel better but when a day starts with one humiliation and is rounded off with another, it's not worth feeling anything.

I slip quietly away to the sanctuary of my room and don't bother to put on the light. It's half-nine and I'm going to bed. Sweet Jesus. I wonder who'll prey on my mind longest tonight. Clare? Matt? Danaher? Or that Icicle With Tits that I was just introduced to?

I've barely flopped in under the duvet when the front door of the apartment is walloped shut by somebody with an almighty urge to be on the other side of it fast. My guess is that it's The Icicle. My other guess is that she and Peter had a blazer over me. They couldn't even have reached dessert.

I just might have done Peter a real favour tonight, but I don't expect him to knock on my door and thank me right away. I'll do him another one tomorrow by going flat-hunting.

# 12

## (CORK)

I'm cradling the pints to protect them from the pressing mob at the bar when I see her. It's the first time I've laid eyes on Clare in six weeks and my heart skips one. Definitely her. She hasn't seen me yet but her eyes are trawling the long, narrow and noisy pub for someone, so it's only a matter of time.

I gingerly ease myself away from the counter, edging and squeezing my way back to Cliffy. He's yelling in some girl's ear and gesticulating wildly with a hand that is holding a full pint. It's spilling everywhere. The dipstick is pissed already.

Cliffy's so engrossed in whatever he's saying to his victim that he's failed to notice that she's looking straight through him and that her mouth is set in a very deliberate sneer. She'll yawn in his face next. Or worse.

I drag him away and the look of relief and gratitude on her face will stay with me for a long time. She even mouths a big thank you at me.

'How could you be pissed already, Gerry, for fuck sake?'

'I'm not. I was flying with your one till you put your oar in.'

Give me patience. How come I got stuck with Gerry Clifford and where the fuck is Jimmy and the rest of them anyway?

Cliffy's looking over my shoulder and then his face lights up. He's seen someone, it must be the lads. What kept the bastards?

'Hiya, Clare? Over here!' He's waving like the village idiot at a passing train.

I don't believe it; the moron couldn't be doing this to me. I poke him hard in the stomach.

'What are you playing at?'

'Relax Dan. You were only going out with her five fucking minutes.'

The urge to punch him full in the mouth is so compelling that I actually make a fist with my free hand. Then she's at my side.

'Hi, Gerry, Dan.' Not even Dan, Gerry.

After all his yelping Clifford is just standing there now, looking from one of us to the other.

'Well, how's life?'

'No complaints, Dan. How's the swotting going?'

I'm trying desperately hard to sound nonchalant, indifferent even.

'Doing a bit here and there, enough to keep the old man off my back.' I study the head on my pint and concentrate on counting the bubbles.

There's this tall, blonde guy standing behind her, dressed like The Osmonds do when they go to the tabernacle. He's smiling at me and I reckon he's a Mormon doing a bit of overtime on a Saturday night.

Clare looks over her shoulder and takes a step back, puts

her arm around his waist and introduces him. A part of me withers and dies there and then.

'This is Greg.'

'Hi,' says Greg, throwing out his hand for it to be shook. I say something but I can't be sure what. Clare explains that Greg's from Boston and is doing pre-med in UCC, staying with relatives in the city.

Gee whiz, that's just swell.

Even Gerry Clifford, the man with half a brain and the wrong half at that, susses that this is an uncomfortable situation and, displaying the sort of lightness of foot that has established him as an out-half of note, he finds space and makes a beeline for the bog.

We make small talk. I ask a few questions about Boston, as if I give a shit, and he replies politely, giving me that Colgate ring of confidence smile. When the well of inanities runs dry we examine each other's shoes, Greg's easily being the shiniest. But you'd expect that from an Osmond.

After another two and half eternities of this, Greg puts his arm around Clare's shoulder, puts down his unfinished glass of lager and says they gotta go.

'Better get this girl home to her mom, Don.'

'Dan.'

'Right.'

If Clare is embarrassed to be seen hanging out with this dork, she doesn't show it. Instead she gives him a squeeze and another part of me withers away. Then they're gone.

Boll. Ox.

I sip my pint, but it tastes of nothing now. It could be herbal fucking tea for all I care. But I don't care. Couldn't care. Couldn't care less.

I have just about made up my mind to call it a night when Jimmy and the gang stream in, announcing that there's a free house up in Sunday's Well and to drink up.

I reluctantly allow myself be persuaded to tag along. Not because I particularly want to, but because I don't want to go home either. I wouldn't sleep. A broken heart will always pound loudest in your ears when you're alone in your bed. It's a well-known fact.

The realisation that Sue Dillon, who has just breezed in looking like a ringer for Jane Fonda in *Klute*, is going along may have influenced my decision as well.

The two of us got on famously when we met at that blow-out I went to the week after Clare and I split up. I didn't make a move then because I was still in official mourning but now that's she's dating an Osmond – well, all bets are off.

The heart might be broken but other parts of me have needs too. At the very least I need a shoulder to cry on. Her shoulders, as it happens, seem particularly sexy and just the job. Tailor-made.

Some party. There's a lo-fi Korean three-in-one music centre in the corner of the room bursting its lungs to make an impression but not getting a fair hearing.

Instead we're being treated to endless choruses of rugby songs from a gang of burly apes who have formed a circle around a crate of beer, their arms draped over each others shoulders. Women are thin on the ground. I haven't a clue who these guys are and I'm happy for things to stay that way.

Haven't an idea whose house I'm in either but it's age-old, rambling and big enough for Jimmy to have got lost in with that skinny one, Deirdre Duffy. I don't know what he sees in her, but then I don't know what she whispered in his ear just before they disappeared either. Whatever it was, it gave him an excuse to try out his infamous leer.

Cliffy is so drunk now that he needs an occasional slap across the face to wake him up. When one is administered, he comes around for a time and rejoins the conversation at the point where he left it fifteen minutes earlier.

This time he's regressed further. Right back to the pub, in fact.

'Cunt,' he says.

'What? Who?'

'That American cunt with your girl.'

'Shut it Gerry. Go back to sleep.' He does, easing himself down the wall and leaning his head against a bookcase. He can stay there this time.

'What's he on about, Dan. Which girl?' Sue is intrigued. I can see by the way her eyes have widened. It's a dismal party and I suppose she wants a bit of amusement. It isn't the sort of amusement that I had in mind but I explain what Clifford was on about anyway, not dwelling on any details.

'I love sorting out people's love lives,' she tells me. 'So start again and don't leave anything out this time.'

I find myself telling her more or less everything but with my own spin on it. Not that she's easily hoodwinked. Occasionally she narrows her eyes in suspicion and I find myself retracting the offending piece of testimony.

When I'm finished, she drags heavily on her cigarette, blows the smoke up to the corniced ceiling like one of those old Hollywood stars and considers the facts as laid out before her.

'She'll be back, Dan. Mark my words. She was just scared off by the whole thing getting so heavy so fast. Couldn't handle it, blamed everyone else and now she's taking stock.'

'And what about Donny Osmond?' I'm the one intrigued now.

'That's the most obvious bit. She knows that she'd meet you sooner or later in the Vin and so she brings along this big hulk to make you jealous.'

'I wish I could believe all that,' I say leaning over to kiss her, 'but thanks anyway.'

Instead of cheering me up, her analysis has just re-opened the wound another stitch or two. Even the thought of this All-American Boy with his arm wrapped around Clare makes me go all clammy.

I make up my mind that I'm going to ring her first thing tomorrow and tell her how I feel. No ifs, buts or brush-offs. I know it's only the drink talking, and very articulate drink at that, but it makes me feel better.

Having shown Sue where it is exactly that I wear my heart, I can hardly start coming on to her now. Anyway, if I was into honesty I'd have to say she's given me no reason to think that she would respond with anything other than a gentle but firm rebuttal. I don't think I'm her type at all. Where do I get these notions from?

We don't have the price of a taxi between us and the walk home will take the guts of an hour. If I was properly jarred this wouldn't bother me one jot but as it is I'm rightly narked.

It also seems to have fallen on me to babysit Clifford all the way to his front door, as Jimmy and that Duffy one have wandered off ahead. I have a strong aversion to drunks, when

I happen to be sober myself, and if you add this to my instinctive aversion to Clifford you have the makings of a very irritating end to a nothing Saturday night.

He's so polluted now that the only way he can make progress is by cautiously easing himself from pillar to post. It's as if he's afraid he'll fall off the edge of the world if he simply stumbles along the footpath.

This will be a particularly difficult procedure from now on because the stout walls along the North Mall are about three foot high and the River Lee is in full spate on the other side of them. Neither Sue nor I have bothered to tell him this.

'If he falls in, let him drown. His mother will thank you, I promise,' Sue tells me, the last of her patience having been spent hauling him away from a hall door that had a very agitated dog on the other side of it.

Jimmy has stopped to talk to a crowd well ahead of us but as we near it becomes obvious that neither he nor the girlfriend are doing any of the talking. When we get nearer still, it becomes clear than Jimmy is being eyeballed by one of them and is being asked would he like to swim home.

I've never being into the physical stuff. My one-liners are often capable of hitting their mark and occasionally I throw a verbal left hook that lands where I want it. Smack. But if heroics are required, I usually turn to the likes of Jimmy. Unfortunately, Jimmy's pinned up to the quayside wall right now and as we get closer still I see only naked terror in his face.

'Shit,' Sue whispers as we approach, and I squeeze her hand.

'No sweat. It will be fine,' I tell her hoping that she can't detect the tremor in my voice. I can.

The guy doing the eyeballing turns his gaze on me. His eyes are bloodshot and take a few seconds to focus on mine. He looks as scary as I imagine any skinhead can. I realise that we're well out of depth, a few nice southsiders snared by six brawl-hardened neanderthals who've been on the look-out for a scrap since closing time.

'Ah, look the cavalry has arrived. Fucking F-Troop . . . '

There's some tittering and Jimmy's girlfriend begins to cry softly, her hands covering her mouth, hoping that nobody will notice.

'Don't worry, Deirdre,' Sue says, trying to reassure her.

'Don't worrrry, Deirdre,' he repeats, mimicking what he imagines she sounds like. This psycho has rubbed his two brain cells together and come to the conclusion that we're privileged little shits who've wandered too far away from our rugger club. I suppose he's half-right.

Clifford has joined us now and he stands there unsteadily as he tries to work out what's going on from behind his personal fog. Psycho's eyes scroll him briefly, before he turns his attention back to me.

'You see, Shit-Head. You don't mind me calling you Shit-Head do you, Shit-Head? You see, me and the lads asked your buddy here for a few fags and do you know what he said. Well?'

I shake my head.

'He said, "Fuck off." Imagine that. "Fuck off," he said. Just like tha'. No, like tha' . . .' Psycho does a Tommy Cooper impression and there's more titters right on cue.

Clifford edges his way up to my shoulder and I can see that he's working himself up to say something, but pray that I'm wrong. I'm not.

'There's a full rugby team following on right behind us, so I wouldn't start anything if I was you, lads.' He points a shaky finger at each of them and then a vacant gaze returns to replace what he must have reckoned was a menacing one.

Thanks Cliffy. Owe you one, old pal. Saved our bacon, all right. Any second now they're going to run back to their shanty towns, evacuating their bowels in sheer terror as they go.

I start to say something when the smallest and stockiest of the gang bursts like a bull from a pen and launches himself at me, head-butting me with such malice and force that it sends me reeling backwards. Before the pain has had time to register I whack the back of my head on the lip of the low wall. There's a dull thud.

I can hear screaming and roaring but it seems some way off and I'm aware that there is a lot of confusion in and around me. Then it seems like I'm being kicked in the balls but oddly it doesn't really hurt. As my body folds itself into a curve, I know that someone else is kicking me in the stomach.


Sue is shaking me by the shoulder and when I open my eyes I can see that she's been crying. Other faces, which I don't recognise, peer gravely at me. When I start to cough my entire body is jolted into a spasm of pain. Somewhere out there too a blue light is flashing. On. Off. On.

'You'll be fine, Dan. I'll stay with you.'

What is she on about? Then I think of something to ask her.

'So you think Clare will be back, do you'?

'What did he say? He said something. What was it?'

Sue is really out of it. Something must have happened. Where's Jimmy anyway? Fucked off with whatshername and left me with Cliffy. Bastard. And my head hurts. It really does.

# 13

## (Dublin)

'Wait till I tell ya.'

Sinead sticks her head around the door of the canteen where I'm dragging the various bits of me together over a cigarette and stewed coffee. Satisfied that we're alone, she flaps a slim file in front of my face and sits down. She couldn't be any more excited if Johnny Depp had phoned to ask her over to LA for the weekend.

'You know your bad loan?'

As if I could forget. 'Danaher wants to see me this afternoon. The little shit knows I'm snookered.'

'No you're not, Dan. Look.'

She throws the file down on the desk in front of me and I flip over the front page. It's a six-year-old assignment on a life policy in the name of a James Burke, the very same shyster who has gone belly-up on me.

'See. We had this as security of an earlier loan on this guy and it's still good today. We have the sucker. You're off the hook.'

'Christ, Sinead, where did you find it? I looked every-where for something like this.'

'A hunch. On some documents he signs himself in Irish,

as de Burca, and some eejit filed him under 'D'. Aren't I a genius?'

'You're a treasure.' I lean across the table and land a big awkward kiss on her blushing cheek. 'You've saved my bacon, Sinead. They were really trying to nail me on this one.'

'Ah,' she waves her hands, embarrassed and surprised at the intensity of my gratitude, 'buy me a drink some time.'

'I will. Tonight, if you're free. Are you?'

'Ya. Why not. Across the road?'

'Great.'

'Grand.'

It's only after the first wave of euphoria and relief has washed over me that I begin to wonder why Sinead has gone to so much bother. Granted, when she joined the branch first I went out of my way to give her a dig out once or twice but only because she used to sit across from me, plucking at her bra strap, on the edge of nervous collapse.

Maybe she remembers those times, or it could be that she simply feels sorry for a pathetic sap who's has lost his wife, son and home and is about to see his modest career do a belly-flop.

There is one other possibility. That is she has always fancied me something rotten and now, knowing that I'm freelance, has decided to try and work her way into my affections. I don't know which cloud that particular fanciful notion floated down from but I can't seem to let go of it. There was something in her expression, or her eyes or something, that gives me a hunch about this.

As I take one last drag on my fag, which will have to sustain me until lunch, I try very hard to disown the notion and concentrate instead on using the live ammo Sinead's given me to turn a disaster into a possible triumph. The meeting, which through sheer cunning and slyness I've managed to have postponed for the past three days, can't come fast enough now.

I meet Canavan as I'm leaving the canteen and he stops just long enough to say that the showdown has been brought forward to midday because Danaher will be out of the office for the afternoon. He switches on the sort of sickly sympathetic look that I thought priests had copyrighted years ago, but he is more than a little taken aback when I volley back an ear-to-ear smile. An ace. Fifteen love.

Sinead sneaks up behind me at the bar and looks over my shoulder. I've been poring over the classifieds in the *Evening Herald*, despairing of finding a decent flat within my budget.

'Are you buying or selling?'

I look up, surprised. 'What do you mean?'

'Well, you're going through the small ads.' It dawns on her then that this might be none of her business and she starts to fluster.

'There I go again,' she says, dumping herself on the nearest stool and letting her handbag drop to the floor.

'Look, if you had being minding your own business earlier I'd be hanging from the branch flagpole this very minute by my sensitive bits. So here's to you.' I raise my pint glass in salute and ask her what she's having.

She can't ask enough questions about the meeting and I tell her how Danaher didn't know whether to be happy that a ten-grand loan hadn't gone bad or mad that I had somehow managed to do a Houdini on him. And how Canavan just sat there looking like a hangman who had been told that the condemned prisoner had been given an eleventh hour pardon.

We're joined by two of the younger staffers who are just in for the one. When they go, I say without conviction that it's time that I headed too but Sinead won't hear of it.

'No. One more. It's my twist. Sit.'

I have the one more and then it's my turn to buy the one more. In no time, all the one mores have added up to a tidy amount and the digital behind the bar that read six-thirty when Sinead plonked herself down is clocking in at nine-thirty.

We seem to be huddled together like co-conspirators now and people ordering drinks give us a wide berth. We swop whispers and nods back and forth and she throws in the odd peal of laughter for the sake of variety.

That's because we're on to her favourite subject, the one she'd specialise in if she ever made it to *Mastermind* – and that's Men.

*Sinead Burke, your chosen subject is Anything In Trousers. You have one minute starting* now . . .

I'd reckon she'd get through an awful lot of questions.

'Will I tell you a little secret, Dan?'

'You might as well. You already know mine.'

'That fiancé I have in Portlaoise Prison doesn't exist. So there. I just made him up to scare off the creeps. Works a treat.'

I do my damnedest to look shocked but most of the lads had worked that out for themselves ages ago.

'Well you didn't threaten me with him once tonight, so that must be good.'

'You're no creep, just the opposite,' she says, looks at me shyly before dropping her eyes to her glass which she has cupped in her lap. She's probably wondering has she made a tactical error.

I don't know what to say next, because I don't know what I want to happen next. If I was asked, as an independent observer, to interpret the nuances of this last piece of conversation, I'd have to objectively conclude that the tired looking guy in the crumpled suit has more than an evens-money chance of pulling the leggy bird with the hair.

But leggy birds with hair were never my type, mostly I think because I was never theirs. Clare was my type. Clare *is* my type. But a fat lot of good that is to me now. Clare is at this very moment snuggling up to Rory Bogtrotter on my couch and guys in hideous jumpers were never her type either.

I excuse myself to go to the loo, just to give myself a chance to contemplate the more important and pertinent questions.

Questions like:

> (a) Is it wise to sleep with someone you work with and who has a reputation for spreading news that is the envy of Rupert Murdoch?
> (b) Does a complicated life like mine really need another complication?

The answer to both these question is a very emphatic 'No!' which is a bit disappointing, so I think of another pertinent question to ask:

> Do I need to get laid in a hurry?

The answer to that one is a resounding 'Yes!' One out of

three isn't bad and I head back to the bar feeling like a predator for a change instead of the bloody victim. But not for long, because Sinead is struggling with her coat when I reach the bar.

'You're not off?'

'I'd better.'

I'm not sure I know what she means and I look at her in such a way that she feels obliged to expand.

'Well, I like you a lot, Dan. But, you know, work and everything . . .'

I wasn't the only one who had been asking themselves questions in the past few minutes.

'It's nobody's business except ours, Sinead.'

I try to get the tone just right and she looks at me hard and steady.

'Are you saying you really like me, Dan, or is it just that you think I'm, well, available? You being on the rebound and everything.'

The drink has made her blunt, but I'm more circumspect. Or, in a word, dishonest.

'Yes, I do really like you,' I tell her. 'I'm not just after what I can get, if that's what you mean.'

I feel like a bit of a heel. But it's what men do in situations like this. Sinead must know so too; whether she'll do herself the favour of admitting as much is not any of my business.

She smiles, but continues to button up her coat. Second last button. Last. It's all slipping away.

'Look, Sinead. How about dinner at the weekend, somewhere nice? No strings attached. How about it?'

If I sound desperate, it's only because I am.

'Ah, why not,' she says after what seems a long time, as if

she feels she's being over-reacting just a little. She throws the strap of her handbag over her shoulder and then she hesitates again. 'Not a word in the office, mind.'

'Another secret, Sinead. A shared one this time.'

Sinead snores. Not those tremendous mattress-tremblers, but she snores nonetheless. I could put it down to the vast quantities of New Zealand Chardonnay she put away, or the hot Masala which she couldn't get enough of.

It wasn't the only thing she couldn't get enough of last night. We were both in such a rush to make a meal of each other when we got back to her flat that clothes were discarded in one of those long trails that I'd only seen in movies that are too chicken to show you the sex.

Lying in her bed as the first of the dusty daylight filters into the room, I'm action-replaying it now, move by move, like a footballer would a particularly good match. I compliment myself on a nice touch there; scold myself for being a tad clumsy somewhere else.

Sinead had made lots of noises but then she's the noisy type. Afterwards she just gave me a quick hug and slid under the blankets and clocked in for her beauty sleep. I nodded off too, happy to have got a game at last; glad to be off the bench.

I thought I might wake up regretting this conquest but to do so would have been to pretend it had just been a late-night impulse caused by a rush of blood and alcohol to the head. In fact, I've been thinking of little else since she walked out of the pub a little unsteadily the other night.

But as soon as good manners allow, I'll be on my way. I'm sure that's what Sinead will want. That way all those nasty complications that situations like this throw up don't have a chance to nest and prosper. Last night was the first night and the final night of our little liaison. By mutual agreement, I'm sure.

I can hear her stirring and feel a tug at the blankets.

'Give me some of them. I'm frozen, you greedy Cork bugger.'

She wraps herself around my back and lifts a warm thigh over mine. I wasn't really expecting this. I had hoped that she could still look me in the eye after last night but it hadn't occurred to me that she might want to take up where we left off.

That's exactly what she does want, manoeuvring her fingers down my tummy to that one part of me that had abstained when it came to a vote on making this a one-night stand.

'Now let me see if Daniel Hayes is an early riser.'

Having established that indeed I am, Sinead burrows deep underneath the bedclothes and starts to do something Clare only ever did on holy days of obligation and not half as well either.

'Where did a nice girl from County Laois learn to do a thing like that?' I ask afterwards, only because I feel I should say something and thanks doesn't seem appropriate.

'In County Offaly,' she replies and laughs so loud that I realise that I have a bit of a hangover.

From now on I'll view the midlands in a whole new light. Sinead Burke likewise.

# 14

## (Cork)

The nurse throws her eyes up to heaven and makes a face as the cranky old fart misreads and then re-reads my chart. He seems puzzled, but then every doctor that's stood at the end of my bed in the past four days has had a vacant look on his face until some passing angel of mercy patiently tells him what's what.

'Nurse, did Mr Sullivan see this chap this morning?'

'He did, doctor. Said the patient could go home to-morrow.' She gives me a wink.

'Well, having seen your various x-rays and whatnot, all I can say is that you're a very lucky young man.'

I nod gravely but I've heard this many times already and it does begin to pale a little on the dozenth telling. Anyway, I can feel another one of those headaches coming on and I could do without the sermon with its sleight-of-hand implication that I must have had a thumping coming.

Surely there must be some old geezer down the ward who'd love to show doctor how his urinary catheter is functioning this afternoon.

When he goes I ask nurse to leave the screen around my bed because I don't think I could face exchanging guff with either the hypochondriac on my left or the dipso opposite who sang rebel songs to himself all of last night. She obliges and says she'll be back in a jiffy to take my pulse and blood pressure.

I'd love to rub that lingering feeling of fatigue out of my eyes but they're much to sore and tender to massage yet, so I close them instead and I'm about to doze off when I hear a very faint hello. When I check I can only see a shadow at the other side of the curtain and the hint of a head peeping tentatively around it.

'Hiya,' the face says, 'are you up to a visitor?'

It must be the painkillers, because it has taken me until now to realise that it's Clare. I cautiously ease myself up and try to smooth down my hair, which hasn't seen a comb since the weekend.

'Yeah, of course.'

I try to sound mildly surprised to see her, but in truth I had fantasised that she'd hear about how I was at death's door, send Donny Osmond back to Salt Lake City and then rush to my bedside begging God to spare me for the sake of our unborn children.

Clare does a second take when she gets close enough to see the state of my face and puts her hand over her open mouth in genuine shock. I like that. Donny would need to have another hit single to compete with this.

'Your face, Dan. Christ.'

She sits ever so carefully on the very edge of my bed, leaving the *NME* and a Toblerone in an Eason's bag on my lap.

'What happened? I've heard all sorts of stories.'

I tell her what I remember and what Sue has remembered for me since. Jimmy got a kick in the face and spent a few hours in casualty; Clifford ran into the middle of the road waving down cars that weren't there and generally cut such a pathetic figure that the gougers eventually took pity on him and left.

'And do you feel as bad as you look?'

'I'm much better today and they're allowing me out tomorrow. The headaches aren't too bad now but the stomach pains from those kicks are still ferocious.'

I lay it on thick as butter, although most of it is true anyway. But I'm not even sure that she's listening any more; instead she seems to have acquired a morbid fascination with my face. She tilts her head this way and that to catch me in the best light.

When I had my first tentative peep in the mirror on Monday, I was fascinated myself. I could see that both eyes had retreated into deep cavities, the immediate area being either purple or otherwise discoloured, and that my nose, although still bandaged, felt crunchy and flat.

'But you'll be all right?'

'Yep. Seemingly. They found brain damage all right but that had been diagnosed by Dirty Harry in first year.'

That husky little laugh again. How I've missed it. How I've missed her.

'So how is Clare Fitz?'

'Fine. All the better for seeing you for myself. I was worried.'

'Were you really? That's nice. Well as you see there's no need.'

We talk of little and nothing, of this and that. She tells me about some classmate who's three weeks late and how she bought the new Wings LP the other day and it's crap. I could have told her. Everything McCartney has done since the break-up has been dire.

For my part, I point in the vague direction of the ward's most revolting character who waved his shrivelled up thing at Matron yesterday and had some vital and vile medical procedure carried out on him soon after. There hasn't been a peep out of him since.

As the tranny on the bedside locker broadcasts the four o'clock headlines, Clare gets up to go and I catch her by the wrist and then let go as quickly. I didn't mean to do that, just did.

'No. Stay a bit. Please.'

She sits down heavily this time and she looks at me for a moment the way she used to. Like she did in Cobh that night two months and three million years ago.

'We've not really talked since that night in your house, Clare. That hasn't been fair. On either of us.'

'I just came into see how you were,' she says, but I can tell she doesn't mean it.

'Sorry,' I say, pretending to be heartbroken, which isn't too difficult to pull off considering that the face registering the hurt is broken already.

'I didn't mean that,' she says, feeling more guilty than she needs to and leaning towards me. 'Is there any part of your face that won't break off if I kiss it?'

'My lips are just fine.'

We kiss lightly but linger a bit. Long enough for me to taste her.

'So who's this Sue then?' Clare asks as she withdraws, keeping her gaze firmly attached to mine, her eyes narrowing. I'm just about to tell her the truth when instinct comes up with a much better answer.

'We've been going out a month or so.'

'Don't hang around, do we?'

'Looks who's talking. What about Donny?'

'Donny? Who's Donny?'

'You know, Donny Osmond. In the Vin.'

'You mean Greg. Poor old Greg. You shouldn't mock the afflicted.'

'The afflicted? You were draped all over him.'

'Was not.'

'Were too.'

'Did it make you jealous, Dan?'

'Course not.'

'Not even slightly?'

'Maybe a little.'

'Well, that's why. He thought it was the Fourth of July and Thanksgiving all at once.'

'Bitch.'

'Suppose so.'

'Does that mean that if I ring you after I get out of San Quentin you'll actually talk to me this time.'

'Depends.'

'On what?'

'On whether you get your good looks back or not. And.'

'And what?'

'And you not dating somebody else.'

Clare knows damn well I won't be. She has it all worked out and not for the first time. This is not merely a mercy visit to the war wounded. It's really her way of letting me know that she's willing to give us another twirl after a respectable interval. No need to involve me in the discussions, of course. All I need to know is that I'm required to turn up at a time and venue yet to be decided.

I should take exception to this cynical and calculated piece of manipulation and wonder if I'm safe in the hands of a girl who is so many steps ahead of me at any one time that I'm sure to get hopelessly lost more than once. But I don't.

'Sue and me? Well, we're more friends really. Like the same sort of movies and stuff.'

Nurse is back now, all hot and bothered.

'Forgot all about you. Sorry. Arm. Out. Good.'

Clare gets up and backs away from the bed, mouthing her goodbyes and then blowing me an exaggerated kiss.

'Thanks for the mag and chocolate,' I shout after her and feel mightily please with myself.

'Is that the girlfriend?'

'Yep.'

It's a wonderful feeling to be able to say that again, even if it is a bit premature.

'Took her time coming in, didn't she?'

Cheeky wagon but then most of these nurses are. No point in being stroppy about it though, otherwise she'll stick up a hose up my rear end and call it a vital medical procedure.

'Ah. She was worth the wait.'

'Love is it, so?'

'Might be.'


I never saw my mother in such a tizzy. She has enough pillows puffed up in my bed to do a harem justice and the electric blanket is registering ten and so hot that if you slipped in a couple of rashers they'd be sizzling in a few minutes.

No matter where my father stands it's the wrong place.

'Will you get out from under my feet, Jack, for the love of God.'

Then he stands somewhere else and it's the wrong place again but he doesn't say a word. Whenever my mother starts clucking and fussing he just backs off and keeps his own counsel. It's that sort of marriage. He's the head of the house and she's in charge.

Coming home from hospital in the car he didn't say much either but I could gather from his demeanour that, yet again, he was far from pleased with his youngest. I had told him exactly what had happened because there was no advantage in telling him anything else, but it didn't seem to make much odds.

My mother told me that he had been on badgering the cops and complaining that things had come to a sorry pass when his son couldn't walk the streets of his own home town. This was her way of telling me that he had been genuinely upset about what happened, although she knows as well as I do that he couldn't say as much. But that's his loss, I'm not pushed either way.

I'm relieved when they eventually leave my bedroom and I carefully lower my sore and sorry frame between the sheets where I start to read an *NME* interview with Iggy Pop. But I can't keep my eyes open and I'm drifting off to sleep when my mother comes back in to tell me that there's someone on the phone for me.

'Tell 'em I'll call back. Who is it? Jimmy?'

'No. It's that nice girl Clare. Such a lovely manner.'

'Oh, I'll take it,' I say and whip off the blankets and lift my legs out of the bed so fast that I forget my damaged bits until a darting pain somewhere in my middle reminds me.

My mother frowns and flaps, but then realises that I'm determined, so she just offers her arm instead.

'I'm fine,' I tell her, which is not the entire truth.

'Well, she must be very special, that's all I can say.'

She is Ma. Trust me on this one.

# 15

## (Dublin)

I should feel abandoned and desolate as I lie on the bed in my new flat. There's very little in this bedroom, except a cheap pine bedside locker, some veneer built-ins and a long narrow window that overlooks a miniature courtyard. But it's mine, or at least it will be as long as I can keep coming up with the rent. That gives me a nice feeling.

I haven't told Clare that I've taken a place yet, though I did tell her that I had exhausted Peter's goodwill over the past eight weeks and it was time to lay my hat somewhere else.

Over at the house to collect Matt at the time, I could see she was a shade taken aback. She realised, I think, as I did, that every decision like this blurs the outlines of our marriage that bit more. But maybe she was just worried about how much it will cost. I could worry about that too but I refuse to. I have to live somewhere and this place is reasonably priced and in a nice part of Dun Laoghaire, close to Shankill and handy for work.

Stretched out, hands behind my head, I find myself pondering a new life on my own without breaking into beads of sweat for the first time. Maybe the opportunities that independence give me are making themselves heard above the tumult at last. Maybe I've come through the worst of it and life won't be a shapeless mess any more. And maybe I should give Sinead a bit of credit too.

We've been seeing and sleeping with each other three or so times a week for the guts of a month and whatever the consequences of that might be in the long term, I'm allowing myself to be spoilt by it at the moment. It's possible that she thinks that this is the relationship that's going to go the distance but I've neither encouraged nor discouraged her in that train of thought.

At this stage it's the company and friendship as much as all that physical exercise that is keeping me curious. That and the fact that she's good fun and thinks I'm cute and witty and clever. After what I've been through, I could do with this outrageous flattery.

Sinead has come up trumps at work too, handling the situation so well that it has crossed my suspicious mind that maybe she's already slept with half the office and came in each of those mornings looking as innocent as she does now.

It wasn't that I worried that she'd drape herself all over my desk and bury my head in her ample cleavage but I was a bit concerned that she might overcompensate, treat me with stony indifference and alert the more sensitive office antennae that way. But I underestimated her and will probably continue to do so.

I feel slightly guilty that I didn't tell her that I was moving in tonight but I wanted to be on my own. This is my place. If she turned up on the first day she might think it was hers too. I'll tell her tomorrow. And Clare.

I'll have to buy myself a cheap CD player and, if I ask

nicely, Clare might allow me take that rarely used portable TV from its perch in the kitchen. Until then the flat will keep its silence and there's nothing for me to do tonight except listen to it. And that suits me fine.

For the first time since this all started my mind seems uncluttered by conflicting thoughts. It's not a mass of contradictions, being dragged this way and that by a thousand warring emotions. The silence of the room plays chaperone to this new-found calm and I wallow in it for what seems a very long time.

My head emptied of all that anger and confusion, I find myself being drawn back to something that has been nibbling away at me for a while. I'm remembering that time a little over three years ago when Clare says it all began to go wrong. Back to that time she badgered me about after we split up. The time, she told me, that she started to leave.

I don't know what's prompting this but this is what my head is filling with. It's as if the time is right for a belated autopsy on a period that might well be at the heart of all our problems. I couldn't have faced this even a fortnight ago; now it seems the most natural thing in the world.

There had been moments when I tried. Slack moments when I was caught off guard and my head trespassed where it shouldn't. Like when I'd queue at the supermarket deli counter, buying a quarter-pound of cooked ham like some lonely old bachelor. I'd find myself wondering how the hell I got to be here at this stage of my life. Or I would be sitting in the traffic or watching something on the telly, when the mind would begin to search and sort through a great clutter of junk memories. But I never allowed myself dwell on them. Didn't dare to.

I could tell where they were leading. To where, to when and why. But I wasn't having any of it. One day at a time, sweet Jesus. That was the motto. A piece of no-nonsense hick philosophy that went to the heart of it. It served me well.

But this is different. I've allowed my head take the lead tonight and I've simply followed. And not only can I recall that period but I can pinpoint the start of our woes to one particular day.

It was suitably wet and wild and Clare was sobbing softly to herself as we drove home from the hospital. I didn't notice at first because of the repetitive swishing of the over-worked wipers as they fought another downpour but little Matt did.

We couldn't tell him why. You couldn't explain to a seven-year-old boy that his mother had a miscarriage three months into a pregnancy that she had waited so patiently for. It could have been the girl that Clare had hoped for too, the girl she had already been calling Sally. I had wanted a second child as well, if only for Matt's sake. Clare's need was a more profound one and it shook her to her core. She was simply devastated.

It was her second miscarriage and even more ugly and traumatic than the first. I tried to spare myself the details, but some had to be absorbed and I felt obliged to ask the doctor some questions, hoping that his answers would be curt and dismissive. Not all of them were.

Damage that had been done when she was having Matt and had come back to haunt us now. The doctor urged a hysterectomy. Sooner rather than later, he said; no point hanging about. He was quite matter-of-fact about it and stole a look at the wall-clock over our heads as he spoke. Next please.

Somewhere between that conversation and that short car journey across south Dublin, Clare's world imploded.

My heart bled for her and for the next week or so I did all the right things. I took time off work; I gave her the hugs; I listened; I kept Matt distracted.

But when the passing weeks were piling high and becoming months, I went back to my normal life. Clare simply couldn't.

Now at night she turned her way in the bed and me mine. Occasionally, I could detect soft tears being smothered in a pillow but I chose not to listen to them. When she sat curled up on the couch vacantly watching the sort of junk television that she was normally allergic to, I pretended that I noticed nothing odd in that either.

I saw a lot and ignored more and even then I was puzzled by how paralysed I was in the face of this crisis. But no matter how often I must have tried to work out the riddle, I never seemed to stay around long enough to come up with a possible solution.

Clare never once reproached me. Never said a word until I went back to the house a few months back to collect some clothes for the first time. Back then my mind was a jumble of crossed wires and I couldn't even begin to untangle. Now I find myself dealing with it without even having to bully myself.

After a year I was convinced that it was all behind us and our friends and her family often remarked how on top of things Clare was. Her mother, a frosty old Cork snob who believed her daughter had sold herself short by marrying me, even gave me a squeeze and said I must have been a great support.

But there's the rub. After that first week of tea and cuddles, I had averted my gaze and spent the next few years fooling myself that things were, or soon would be, fine. Some support. All the while, Clare was trapped in a nightmare. When I wasn't there to coax her out of it, she found someone who was.

I must have had all this worked out before now, but I hadn't allowed myself to acknowledge it. It might even be that I'm being too hard on myself but after endless weeks of blaming anybody and everybody for the whole mess, it might do me some good to have a long, hard look in the mirror. At the moment there's a guilty man staring right back and all he's short is a convict number hanging around his neck.

The silence that drew all this out of me has stared to intimidate me now, so I slip on my jacket and decide to try out the pub around the corner. I've confessed enough for one night and in the absence of absolution, a few pints of porter will have to do.

Sinead turns up at my door the following night sitting on a biggish box and quite obviously out of breath.

'Christ, I should have waited for the lift. That thing weighs a ton.'

'What is it?'

'A little moving-in present. Go on, open it.'

I drag it inside and tug at the stubborn staples. Tucked in between two slabs of polystyrene is a portable television.

'For me?'

'No stupid, it's for the guy next door.'

'Christ. Thanks, Sinead. But it's too much, really.'

'Don't be silly. But I would love a little hug.'

She holds me in a tight squeeze for long enough for me to wonder if this is just a housewarming present or some sort of down payment. Cynical and ungracious maybe but I don't want her buying into my life, simply because none of it is for sale. Whenever I seem to catch up with all the changes in my chaotic little world, something else seems to get ahead of me.

'Can I stay over?' she asks, smiling and catching me unawares.

'Of course.'

I somehow camouflage my unease when I give this reflex response. But when she begins to caress my back in that way of hers, the unease quickly burns itself off and I suspect that I may be for sale after all. Bargain basement price too.

'Plenty of time for that later,' she says untangling herself once she realises that she's pressed one button too many. 'I'm starving.'

'I'll get a takeaway delivered. Indian? Chinese? Pizza?

'Pizza will do fine.'

I phone in our order, unbox the TV and spend the next half-hour trying to decode the tuning instructions. Sinead, having already done an approving tour of inspection, is stacking enough toiletries in the bathroom to do her until the next millennium and that sense of unease is back again, perched menacingly on my left shoulder.

'You don't mind? Better than dragging an overnight bag every time.'

'Sure,' I say, not trying too hard to disguise my feelings this time. But Sinead is humming away to herself and not listening out for an answer, least of all one with a negative sting in its tail. The Icicle with Tits turned Peter's bathroom into occupied territory too and never came back to collect any of it after storming out that night. But no need to panic. Not yet anyway.

The doorbell goes and I leap up to answer.

'It's our dinner. I'll get it.'

But when I open the door I don't find the pizza-man. Instead my eyes fall on a beaming Matt and, two paces behind him, his mother, carrying a portable TV trailing a long lead. Shit. It takes me a while to think of anything to say, by which time Matt has thought of loads and is already in the living-room.

'I brought you this brill Liverpool poster for your bedroom. It's cool. Have you got thumbtacks? Wow, this place is fabulous. Isn't it, Mum?'

Mum is looking at me a bit oddly and waiting for me to take the TV, which I eventually do.

'Oh come in. And thanks.'

'When I told Matt you rang he said he couldn't wait for the weekend. He had to see the place, you know what he's like. So we brought the portable as requested.'

Sinead has emerged from the bathroom and is standing behind Matt, not knowing where to put herself. She eventually decides to stay where she is and tries to smile, but the corners of her mouth refuse to conform and she just looks ever more out of place.

Matt and Clare notice her at the same time and there's an awkward silence that I feel obliged to break.

'Clare. This is Sinead. Sinead . . . Clare. Sinead's just dropped in for a bite to eat and to help me settle in.'

'Oh.' says Clare, who appears astonished but is telling herself that she has no right to be.

I introduce Matt to Sinead, but by now his attention has by now been drawn to the state-of-the-art portable in the corner.

'You already have a telly, Dad.'

'I know. A mix-up. Sorry.' I put the other one down and ask Clare to take a pew, but she declines. Thank God for small mercies.

'No. We'd better be off. Come on Matt.'

'But we just got here.'

'Would you like a cuppa or something, Clare. Glass of vino?'

She shakes her head. I can tell she really wants to be out of here.

'How about you come over and help me settle in on my first weekend, Matt?'

I'm cutting a deal with him and he knows it and his face brightens. But he looks hard at an increasingly fidgety Sinead, as if wondering if she'd be around to spoil it.

'Just the two of us.' I give him a wink.

'Are you getting in Sky Sport?' He drives a hard bargain.

'Why not.' I'll say anything, just so this chalice will pass.

Clare is scanning all five foot ten inches of Sinead, making absolutely sure she doesn't miss a thing. I know her well to enough to guess that she'll have Sinead marked down as a bit of fluff. Truth is, up to three weeks ago, I would too.

'I'll see . . . see you to the car.'

Sinead tries her best at a cheery goodbye, Clare does the

minimum in return and Matt ignores the little ritual completely.

We're outside and at the car before another word is spoken and, with Matt busy securing his seat belt, Clare comes right out with it.

'So how long have you been sleeping with her?'

She puts undue emphasis on that last word, which is enough to let me know that she doesn't approve at all. I'm pleased about that.

'You're jumping to conclusions, Clare.' I feel a token denial is the least I can offer.

'No I'm not.'

'Well, if you must know, not long. Long after we split up, if that's what you're asking. Anyway, it's nothing serious.'

'Just sex?' A straight question.

'More or less.' A straight answer, more or less.

'Does she know that?'

'Sinead's not stupid.'

'She works in your branch, doesn't she? I remember her from one of those awful bank piss-ups I used to be dragged to occasionally.'

'You do?'

'Yep. She was out of her tree singing 'Patricia The Stripper' on a table in the pub. All legs and tits.'

She could have added 'and no brains' but the implication was so obvious she didn't have to. I would be livid over Clare's casual callousness if there was anything personal in it. But there's not, this is still about Clare and me. Sinead is just an innocent bystander.

We're standing close now to make sure that Matt won't

overhear and I can't resist running the back of my hand lightly down her left cheek. For the few seconds that it takes, she lets her head lean that way and looks at me with big watery eyes. Maybe it's just the start of a head cold.

'We've probably made a huge mistake, you know, Clare. Breaking up.'

'Well, that mistake can join the queue with all our other ones and wait in line. I'll ring you to make arrangements for the weekend. Nice flat. Got to go.'

Back to earth with a thump.

I give Matt the thumbs up, Clare turns over the motor and they're away but the car hasn't gone far when the reversing lights come on and Clare back-tracks, sticking her head out the window.

'Forgot to tell you,' she shouts, 'Jimmy rang from London. He's coming to Dublin for some rugby international in two weeks. I gave him your new number.'

Not sure I'm up to that just yet. Flynnie still behaves like a sixteen-year-old who's just discovered girls and drink. That comes from never having settled down and nobody being there constantly to remind him of his responsibilities and demand money with menaces.

I take my time strolling back to the flat and wonder if Sinead has recovered enough of her composure to remember to open the red and let it breathe.

# 16

## (KINSALE)

It's midnight and I'm stretched out on the pier and looking up at the stars. I can hear footsteps on the rickety planks behind me but I can't be bothered to turn around. I know it's Clare. I'd know that soft footfall anywhere.

'So this is where you got to,' she says, slurring her words slightly and sitting down heavily next to me. 'Are you sure you're all right?'

'Feel nicely pissed. Not wild pissed, more mellow. Had a wee joint too, you see. Different vibe completely.'

'Weird.' She's lying down now too but looking at me instead of the skies. 'I thought I'd have to hire a JCB to dig you out of the pub tonight. Three honours and everything. Better than you expected.'

There's a whole busload of us in Kinsale to celebrate the Leaving Cert results. They'll pile out of the pub and on to the town's quaint little streets any minute now and the place won't know what hit it. I came out here half an hour ago because I wasn't drunk enough to enjoy the celebrations at the level they'd reached.

Needed some air. Needed to be alone.

Clare is silent for a long time, because she knows that to

rabbit on would be an intrusion, but then she can't contain herself any longer. I even have an idea of what's coming

'So what are you going to do, Dan. Go to college?' Clare has been circling around this subject all evening and I have been hedging my bets but I suppose she deserves to have an inkling. Not that I have much of an inkling myself.

'And do a BA? Can you see me as a teacher?'

'What then?'

'Like I've said, I'd like to get out of home. That's a priority. Maybe the bank or something. Dublin would be the biz. Maybe London.'

'I can't imagine you in a suit and being polite to old dears.'

'It's only as a way out and to put a few bob in the pocket until I really grow up and decide what I want to be. A means to an end. A meal ticket.'

'And what about me?' She throws this in so casually that it would be easy to believe that she doesn't care too much either way. But I know better by now.

'You and me will be fine. I promise. Let's just wait and see. Besides, you'll have your head stuck in the books from now on. It's your turn next year.'

I can't be more specific than that, simply because I genuinely don't know what I want, except I know that I want Clare. That's taken as read by me. Keeping her guessing a little is good for the soul. My soul.

It's a balmy August night but there's a light chill in the sea breeze now and Clare cuddles up to me and gives a little shiver. I could tell her I love her now, but I won't. Lying underneath a twinkling sky like this and saying words like that would just be too much, so I give her a squeeze instead, which she can interpret any way she wishes.

I can hear a glass smash on some nearby street. That's followed by howls of laughter, someone singing 'The Men Behind The Wire' and what sounds like a car bonnet denting under trampling size tens. On cue, the pier vibrates to a stampede of thundering feet.

Jimmy is being carried, flailing and yelping, by Moss Barrett, Gerry Clifford, Murph and some other idiot whom I can't make out in the dark. They seem intent on tossing their gyrating cargo over the side and into the mucky low tide, but they think better of it and dump him unceremoniously on the ground instead.

Thud.

Then they collapse in a drunken heap, laughing helplessly.

'I know.' says Jimmy, getting up on his feet unsteadily, tucking in his shirt and doing a passable Long John Silver impersonation, 'Let's set sail on the high seas, me hearties.'

They all laugh again but when Jimmy's this pissed and has that glint in his eye, anything is possible. There are no impossibles for him on a night like this.

I've counted myself out even before he's asked, but it's not at all certain that he'll press-gang me anyway. Ever since we took that hiding on the North Mall there's been a certain coolness between us. Nothing said or even hinted at but it's there all the same.

My hunch would be that his pride was hurt because I was the one that got the serious pasting. Bizarre, but Jimmy's like that. He has to be the centre of things, even if it means being the victim the odd time. Either that or he's harbouring guilt over the fact that he was stupid enough to tell those cretins to fuck off in the first place.

I wasn't destined to see that much of him after that anyway. Clare had chalked off a big bit of me for herself. Having lost her once, I wasn't complaining. The old man chalked off the bulk of the remainder in the cause of academic achievement.

That left very little time for pissing into petrol tanks and swigging brandy at discos.

'Who's on?' Jimmy asks.

They're all on, of course, and without as much as a sideways glance at me or Clare he leads them down the longest of the floating marinas and we watch until the five of them seem to merge into one and then disappear from view entirely.

'This should be hilarious,' says Clare sitting up now and bringing her knees up to her chin. She lights a ciggie for herself and one for me.

'That's if they don't all drown. Jimmy knows about boats but those other dorks have never even had a bath.'

Somebody's shouting at us from the street.

'The bus is heading back at one. Sharp.'

We decide to give it a while and our patience is rewarded when a wavering dingy drifts into the slipstream of a marina light.

'Would you look at them . . . '

We can make out the stark shape of one lanky, curly-headed figure standing with more confidence than balance and using a single oar slowly and gently to guide the groaning craft to shore.

His crew is sitting perfectly still, grimly clutching the sides and trying to do a Rod Stewart with 'Sailing'. Some know the chorus; others not even that.

It's strange sitting here and spectating at the sort of lark that I've often been in the thick of. For a moment I regret not being out there with them, because there may not be too many more nights like it. Maybe none at all.

I train my eyes on the boat and at first I think the moonlight is playing tricks but when Clare grabs me by the arm, I allow myself believe that the boat is really tilting dangerously to one side. The suspicion is confirmed when someone cries out.

'Jesus! O mother of divine shite. I can't swim.' It must be Cliffy. Just the guy to have around in a crisis.

Then, after what appears a long interval of silence and stillness, the boat lurches violently to the left and scuttles its unscheduled freight into Kinsale Harbour in one grand gesture.

I watch hypnotised as the five of them frantically grab at each other and the upturning boat. Their roars and wails are loud enough to raise the *Lusitania*.

'Do something, Dan! For Christ sake.'

Clare is standing now and looking down at me in disbelief. But by the time I get to my feet, danger has given way to farce. Because instead of splashing frantically about, or drowning with dignity, they're just standing there, the lapping waters barely reaching their waists, looking very sombre, sober and wet.

All, that is, except Jimmy who has managed to clamour on to the slippery bottom of the boat and is, for reasons best known to himself, singing 'Rule Britannia'.

*Britannia rules the waves . . .*

The sullen coach driver finally cranks his old jalopy into gear at a few minutes to two after grudgingly conceding that Long John Silver and his soaking midshipmen are entitled to get on the bus with the rest of us. The roar that greets them as they squelch their way to the back of the bus is almost as loud as the one they themselves made when they were dumped into the Atlantic.

'Have a good look around,' Clare tells me as the bus weaves his way around the bends home. 'You won't see a lot of these guys for a long time again.'

I nod but I don't bother to open my eyes.

'But I'll be seeing you tomorrow, won't I?'

'Suppose so.'

'Well, that will do me.'

# 17

# (Dublin)

Jimmy's never lost it. Right now he's up at the nightclub bar exchanging very rude body language and mouth-to-ear intimacies with two gorgeous young creatures half his age who are wearing too much make-up and very little of everything else. Fair play to them.

Maybe it's that accent, which has a lot of London mixed in with that ingrained Deep South purr. Or it might be those long and ludicrous sideburns. Whatever it is, Flynnie has it in spades and the undeniable knowledge that he's hurtling towards middle-age at the speed of light doesn't seem to bother him a jot.

He returns to our table with two bottles of designer beer and slides himself on to the long seat, throwing his feet up on the one opposite and shouting in my ear to be heard over the thumping dance music.

'Those two are game for anything. Another night perhaps.'

'What time is it?'

'Nearly one.'

'Christ, I'm pissed. I'm well out of practice.'

'Too much shagging. What's her name?'

'You mean Sinead?'

'Ya. Her. Not that I can believe that you and Clare have split up. When Clare told me on the phone I was speechless. Honestly. Struck dumb.'

I had gone through it with Jimmy over the first few pints in Mulligans and, although he frowned at all the candid parts, it was obvious that he couldn't really fathom it. But then, that's what I'd expect from a veteran solo artist.

When Jimmy packed in art college in Cork and decided to take his chances in London, I honestly thought that our old friendship, which has been strained over the previous year or so anyway, would fade out like any one of a hundred hit singles. We seemed to have outgrown each other at the same time, me going my way and Jimmy his. But the opposite happened.

Instead, he made a point of being in regular contact. I started getting the odd phone call, usually from a noisy pub. Then there followed scribbled postcards and, occasionally, quickly dashed-off cartoons, just like the ones he used to covertly pass around class.

They were juvenile. Rude and hilarious.

Now a bit of a noise at some advertising agency, Jimmy is still the one who makes the effort to stay in touch, although the recent upheavals in my life have given me a credible excuse for dereliction of duty.

He jumps up suddenly.

'Fuck this miserable shite,' he says holding up his lager. 'I'll get us a couple of bottles of wine. Can't wake up on the morning of an international without a humdinger of a hangover, now can we?'

'It's my twist,' I tell him and I edge my way to the bar and dig a hole for myself in the dead centre of it, waving my money at the barman until he takes notice. Jimmy's right. No point in getting slightly sauced. A sheep and a lamb and all that.

We pour the overpriced rotgut down our throats in no time, doing our best to bypass our palates. Then we get in two more bottles of the same in the one excursion to the bar, just to round things off. Before another hour or so has passed we're engrossed in the sort of conversation that flits from the shallow and witless to the deep and personal without the benefit of any sort of recognisable pattern.

One head supporting the other by the forehead, Jimmy looks into my eyes and I can sense advise coming on. He used to do this sort of thing all the time in the old days. It used to really irritate me then as well.

'Now, don't get me wrong, Danny baby. But do you know what I think?'

'Think about what?'

'About you and Clare.'

'No,' I say, yawning into his face and hoping against hope that he'll take the hint. But I know he won't.

'You see. You got involved with each other too young. You and her. I mean, what the fuck does anyone know about anything at eighteen?'

'If I recall correctly, at eighteen Jimmy Flynn thought he knew fucking everything.'

I stick a finger in his chest and spill some wine down his shirt. He doesn't notice or else he doesn't care.

'Only how to pull birds and piss in letterboxes, that's all. That's all we knew.'

'I reckon you'll still be pulling them when you're collecting your pension from Her Majesty, Jimmy.'

'Believe me, that gets boring too. It's just that I'm too fucking old to change now. If I sleep with a woman for more than a couple of weeks I start to panic in case she wants to move in or something.'

That's the closest to being fallible and vulnerable that Flynnie has ever come to in my company. Instead of telling me how falling in love too young ruined my life, he's hinting instead that not being able to fall in love at all might now be blighting his.

God's gift to women has lost the plot. Now there's a thing. Almost makes me feel good.

He falls silent, picks up the third bottle and gives it a shake to see if there's another liquid ounce in it. I could dearly love to tease this out a while longer but I'm not at all sure that, at this stage of the evening, I'm capable of teasing out anything more complex than my address.

'Come on, Jimmy. Enough's enough. Let's see if we can get a taxi.'

The frozen revellers waiting at the taxi rank in Stephen's Green have clotted into twos and threes, huddled against vindictive sleet showers which seem to be racing up the street rather than raining from the skies.

Jimmy pats the breast pockets of his jacket and then slips in a fumbling hand. It emerges holding a hip flask in a tattered crocodile case.

'Remember this?'

'No,' I say, because monosyllabic answers are the only ones that I feel confident of getting away with.

'Course you do,' he says and screws off the silver top and hands it to me. 'Remember when I used to nick it from the old lad and we'd both get polluted on brandy at the rugby disco? Innocent times.'

I smile in belated recognition and, for old time's sake, take a generous swig.

'The very one?'

'The very one. Never go to an international without it. It goes to White Hart Lane every other Saturday too. When Da died, I took it as a keepsake.'

We fall silent then, trying to shrink into our coats to escape the weather and by the time we're at the top of the queue and our taxi comes I find myself leaning on Jimmy for support.

'I'm fine,' I tell him as I blunder my way into the back seat but as soon as the doors are closed and the warm, stale air of the car heater fans my face I know that I'm not well at all.

I can hear Jimmy and the taxi driver talk and then feel a lurch as the car speeds off the blocks and swings right up the Green. I concentrate hard on not being violently ill, wind down my window a piece and lay my heavy head against the headrest.

After what feels like a very long time I can hear the car door creak open and I open my eyes when Jimmy gives me a shake on the shoulder.

'Come on, we're home. Can you stand?'

I take immediate offence and make a supreme effort and just about manage it.

'Steady,' he says, as if I'm tilting this way and that for the fun of it. Jimmy slams the door, the taxi speeds off and I throw an elaborate farewell wave in its wake.

I stand on the pavement for a full minute trying to dig out the door keys before I realise that not everything is as it should be. Or where it should be. Like my flat, for instance.

'Jimmy,' I say, because I don't really trust my senses at times like this, 'where the fuck are we?'

'What do you mean "Where are we?"' he says, offering me more brandy and looking at me with eyes that could do with being shut down for at least twelve hours.

I know where we are, all right, and what I should really be asking Jimmy is why we are here.

In Shankill.

Where I used to live and where Clare and Matt still do.

'I mean, old son,' I tell him, 'this is where I *used* to fucking live. But not where I live now. Not where you dumped your bags this afternoon, now is it?'

It dawns of him, at last, as he slowly takes in his surroundings. He even has a look at the sky, as if that's going to tell him anything. Tosser.

'Oh shit,' he says. 'Bollox. I just gave the taximan the wrong address. Sorry. Oh fuck.'

I'm not so drunk that I don't feel uncomfortable hanging around outside my old home. I can sense the eyes of a hundred neighbours on my back. I can hear a thousand tut-tuts.

'Let's get out of here, Jimmy. You're a total wanker, do you know that?'

'Right,' he says, as if he'd do anything to please me now. 'But I gotta take a leak first. Nature demands it.'

It's only now that I've noticed Rory Bogtrotter's Golf parked outside, with two wheels up on the grass verge and dried cowshite congealed along the side. He must have been home to see the mammy recently.

Jimmy follows my stare.

'Is that the fucker's car?' He sounds incredulous, as if he's never screwed a married woman in his life.

I say nothing, which is all the evidence he needs. Before I have time to work out what he's trying to do, Jimmy undoes his zip, lifts the hinged petrol flap and furiously tries to force the cap itself, which is securely locked.

'Jesus, Jimmy. No!'

The porch light has come on and I can see the net curtains in the bedroom flutter. That will be Mrs Bogtrotter.

Then the front door swings open violently and Mr Bogtrotter storms down the drive carrying Clare's hockey stick. As if eighteen again, we both bolt up the park, with Jimmy trying to shove his lad back where he got it from.

'Get in, ya whore . . . '

Before we take a left that will take us out of the estate, but still within earshot of the house, Jimmy turns, points and bellows:

*'You're going home in a fucken ambulance!'*

Presumably this is what they shout at White Hart Lane when Arsenal visit. I could have done without that too. If by some fluke, Clare didn't recognise who was hanging around the drive, there's very little chance she'd mistake Flynnie's hybrid accent for anybody else's.

Boll. Ox.

In this snakes-and-ladders life of mine, I reckon I've just slithered back down to square one.

I'm the one dragging Jimmy now. That last swig of brandy was obviously one too many for him.

But there's no point being mad when we're both too drunk to either articulate or respond to anything. Anyway, I need my remaining few grams of energy to walk us both as far as the village to phone a cab.

Plenty of time to be mad in the morning.

# 18

## (CORK)

My hands are still shaking when I pick up the receiver and dial the one number I know off by heart. I had planned to ring Clare anyway, around the time she finished dinner and before she got stuck into the books, to tell her that I had got the bank and wasn't it bloody brilliant.

But I'm ringing her to tell her something else now, something so traumatic that three hours after I have witnessed it, I still can't get my hands to be still.

Clare answers herself. She knows that I'm expecting a letter from the bank today and she's eager for news. At the last interview they told me that they'd be in touch by the middle of next week and that's today, or thereabouts.

'Hi Clare.'

'Oh hiya. Any word?'

I don't say anything for whatever reason but probably because I'm afraid I might break down and make a fool of myself.

'Hello? Dan?'

Nothing.

'You still there?'

All she can hear is my breathing, which is a bit erratic. I

take a deep breath, holding my hand over the mouthpiece. That's a bit better.

'Dan. Talk to me, for Christ sake.'

'Sorry,' I say and sniffle loudly.

'Was it bad news from the bank?'

'No.'

'Jesus, Dan. Talk.'

'It's the da.'

'Not another bust-up.'

'No. He's dead. Today. Massive heart attack.'

Clumsy, but it's out now.

'Oh Christ, Dan. I'm so sorry. You poor thing.'

I tell her, without being asked, exactly what had happened. How I came in the front door without a care in the world and how my mother grabbed me by the sleeve and pulled me into the living-room. The da was crouched on the floor, leaning against his armchair. His face was ashen, he was making very shallow gurgling noises and his eyes were rolled back in his head. I had never seen anyone dying before but I knew my father was dying in front of me then.

I told my mother to keep talking to him and I rang our doctor, cleared the fence into our neighbours and banged on the door looking for the nurse who lodges there. By the time I got back into the room he was already gone. There was an unmistakable stillness about him. The priest would later say that he looked peaceful but then he would say that.

I sat there looking at my father for what seemed like for ever. I told myself that he had been pleased this morning about the job.

But I knew too that he had really wanted me to go to college and get a degree. We had a few bitter spats over that recently, after I had told him that I wanted away from Cork and him too. Things were said then. And not all of them by me either.

I buried my face in my hands and rubbed at my eyes furiously as if trying to wipe away these flashbacks. When I looked across at him again, he was no longer my dad. He had become a corpse and I had to leave the room.

I tell Clare all this and I know I have to see her later.

'Can you get away for an hour? A walk. I need the air.'

'Okay. Sure.'

In another while the house is full. The business of death is like any other and for it to be observed, relatives, friends and neighbours feel they have to come knocking softly on your door. Once over the threshold, they go about their duties employing suitably hushed tones and offering tea and consolation to those who wish for it and even those who don't.

They're not the only ones who come bearing sympathy. There are priests, doctors and undertakers to contend with too, but being the youngest I'm largely ignored by these professionals and this gives me the perfect opportunity to give this circus of the macabre the slip for a few hours.

I've gone out with Clare many times in the past months and I've looked forward to seeing her each time. But this is the first time that I've actually needed to see her. This quantum leap isn't lost on me, even on a night like this when my emotions are scattered all over the place like car bomb debris.

We don't say much as we walk along the Marina from one boatclub to the other in the comforting dusk. The path along by the River Lee is a carpet of crunchy autumn leaves and instead of talking I concentrate on shunting them along in front of me. I must look like a sulky little boy who's being dragged home for his tea by his mother but the repetitiveness of it has become a welcome distraction.

I have little I want to add to all that I told Clare over the phone and she is content to stroll alongside me, her arm locked into mine. It's only when we stop to follow the progress of a rowing crew, battling wind and current, that I become conscious of how long it has been since I offered a morsel of conversation.

'It hasn't been all misery today.'

'Oh?'

'I got a letter from the bank this morning. They've offered me a job.'

'Brilliant,' she says excited but not really letting on. 'I knew you'd get it.'

'I have to go for training now and at the end of that they'll post me somewhere. God only knows where. Some place with a bit of life hopefully.'

'Fingers crossed for Dublin, Dan, if it's what you want.'

It is, I think. It was the last time I looked. I'll look again soon. But not today, tomorrow or this week. She seems to understand that and says no more.

Our eyes follow the pencil-slim craft for a little longer and then we turn our backs on the river and its struggling oarsmen and head towards home. I feel the better for having met her tonight and when we reach her gate I tell her so and a bit more besides.

'I'm in love with you, Clare. As if you hadn't guessed.'

'I'm a bad guesser. I'm glad you told me.'

There's a silence, the sort that would be awkward at any

other time, but not now. We hug and say our goodnights.

I take my time walking the rest of the way home, having already imagined what awaits me when I turn the key in the front door. There'll be pots of tea, plates of sandwiches and my mother will have brought out the Bristol Cream and that bottle of Power, the one that had its seal broken last Christmas and has had dust settling on it since.

Kevin and Sheila will glare at me but won't bother to ask where the hell I've been and my mother will tell Auntie Eileen that I was offered a place in the bank this very day. Auntie Eileen will gush how proud that will make my father, who's looking down from heaven and praying for us.

Yes, my mother will say, fidgeting with a tea-towel and beaming at her three children through tear-stained eyes, he was very proud of all of us.

Lies, damned lies and a mother's lies.

At that point I'll say how tired I am, take one of the remaining ham sandwiches and excuse myself. Then I'll go to bed and try to remember how Clare's face lit up when I told her I loved her and try to forget that corpse on the floor, the one that used to be my father.

# 19

## (DUBLIN)

I stare at him blankly and can't think of anything to say at first. Eventually, I take a step back and mumble an invitation for him to come in, which he accepts by brushing past me.

Not many people drop by my flat, simply because not a lot of people know that I live here yet. That suits me just fine, especially after this survival course of a weekend. Jimmy flew back to London this afternoon and much and all as I enjoyed his visit, I enjoyed watching his broad back disappear into Departures even more. Too much of a good thing.

My plan for this Sunday evening is to stretch out on the couch with the papers and then crash around ten. At least that was my plan, until he showed up.

'What can I do for you, Rory?' I ask, trying to set my voice somewhere between politeness and hostility, but it comes out sounding like I'm nervous and narked, which is closer to the truth.

'Just thought we should get a few things straightened out,' he says looking around the room like a detective might a crime scene. Maybe he's looking for something to hit me over the head with.

'Like what exactly?' I don't bother to offer him a seat

and I don't close the door either. No point in making him feel welcome when he's not.

'Well, I don't want to have to look over my shoulder every five minutes to check if you and your buddies are about to vandalise my car.'

He means Friday night, of course, and I smirk as if the incident is dimly remembered and of no particular consequence.

'Look, we were well pissed; got the taxi to the wrong house and Jimmy started messing. That's all. No malice aforethought.'

He looks at me long and hard. The Rory I'd moulded into shape in my head doesn't look at people like that. I have him down as a big soft rural lug who wears bad sweaters. The guy looking at me now is wearing an offensive sweater all right – an XL brown Fair Isle to be precise – but the stare that refuses to let up could only be owned by someone who has a harder edge. Bully for him.

'So it won't happen again?'

'Suppose not,' I say, arms folded and staring him back every bit as hard, promising myself that I won't be the one to blink first.

'Well, that's fine then,' he says, surprising me again by working himself up to a tepid smile and relaxing his shoulders, like a soldier at ease. He had obviously wound himself into a state on the drive over here and I could almost feel sorry for him. Could, but I don't.

'Did Clare put you up to this?'

'Christ, no. And don't tell her either. She didn't even know that you and a mate were causing the bother the other night. She just thought it was a couple of drunk youngsters on their way home.'

'And what did she say when you told her?'

'I didn't.'

'Fair fucks, that was decent. I was dreading ringing her, to be honest.'

I'm genuinely impressed and bordering on the grateful. I shut the door and offer him a seat, which he clears of scattered newspapers and slowly drops himself into.

'Look,' he says, jangling car keys in his hands, which would appear to be something of a nervous habit. 'I can't imagine how rough this has all been on you. If I was in your position I'm sure I'd react just the same. Worse maybe. That's all I wanted to say.'

Me being nice to him. Him to me. At least it seems so, unless I'm missing something.

I wander into the kitchen to get a couple of cans from the fridge and to give me myself a few precious seconds to get a handle on this unscheduled but revealing visit. He doesn't seem the devious sort and as it appears that Clare hasn't put him up to anything, I allow myself to relax and work out the best way of saying something to Rory that's been on my mind a while and which I may not get the opportunity to sound him out on again.

I toss the cold Heineken to him and we sit facing each other for a few moments busying ourselves with the mechanics of levering open the cans and taking the first frothy mouthfuls. Man stuff. We could even be mates about to settle down to watch the footie on the box.

I decide where to start and see where it takes me.

'So you and Clare are for the long haul, you reckon?' I keep my eyes on his and then fill my mouth to bulging with more beer, swishing it around like mouth wash.

He looks at me surprised, thinks about not answering at all and then does with a shrug and, looking around again, opts to change the subject.

'Not a bad little pad. Great location. A stroll from the pier. Lovely.'

I agree and then boomerang the conversation right back to where it came from.

'It's just that I have to think about Matt, you know and his future. It's been tough for the little man.'

This is not the sort of thing he came to talk about and I know that I have only until he finishes that beer to prise anything out of him. He takes a long swig, glances at his watch and nods gravely, knowing he has to say something.

'I'm not trying to be a substitute dad or anything, Dan. I'm rarely there in fact, and then it's mostly weekends when Mattie's over here.'

I ignore the Mattie and continue as if he hadn't spoken at all.

'What worries me is something he said to me a few weeks back – and this is between you and me.'

'Okay,' he says but he's perched at the edge of his seat now and wishing he was anywhere else. He came to make a point and I can tell he's sorry he didn't quit when he was ahead.

'Well, Matt was concerned about you and Clare starting a family. He was very confused about it. I told him it was ridiculous.'

'Certainly jumping the gun there all right. That's well down the road I'd imagine, if ever.'

'Well, as you know, Rory. There is no road.'

He puts the beer can down on the coffee table, allowing a frown to settle on his face. Rory doesn't know exactly what I mean yet but he can guess it's not going to be something he wants to hear.

'What do you mean there is no road?

'Well, that Clare can't have any more kids, of course.'

'Sorry?'

I can tell from the shock that has registered in his voice and the way he's had to clear his throat, that this is the first he's heard of it. Clare presumably told him about the miscarriages but not about the heartbreak medical advice that followed the second one. Ever since Matt's tearful outburst in Eddie Rockets, I've had a inkling that this was the case.

Bingo.

'You mean you didn't know. That Clare never told you?'

I say it quietly, almost sympathetically, carefully sifting out any trace of triumphalism before I speak.

He starts to say something, stutters over a few words, fumbles with his keys some more, bids me a curt goodnight and leaves, shutting the door quietly behind him. A touch of dignity there, I'll give him that.

Rory, who won't see forty again unless the gods decide to reincarnate him, has obviously put a lot of store in the idyllic notion of belatedly starting a family with this woman he's been lucky enough to woo away from a careless, inattentive husband.

For her part, Clare couldn't bring herself to tell him that she couldn't give him this family, for fear of hurting him or losing him. Or possibly both.

Clare is her own women. Mrs Fucking Independent.

Brushed me off like she might crumbs from her lap. Dismissively. With a careless wipe of the back of her hand.

Deep down, though, I reckon she was a bit scared. Scared of rearing Matt on her own. And of his growing up and then moving on. She mightn't need me right now but she needs somebody. Somebody big and cuddly like Rory. Somebody to wrap around herself around on a winter's night and wake up next to on a summer's morning.

If Rory takes our conversation to heart, he could well be reversing his faithful Golf out of my drive this very night. Quicker than you could say 'Serves you right, asshole!' Or words to that effect.

And that would make Clare scared all over again and wondering how she could screw up so badly.

I'm guessing, of course and maybe it's all too neatly packaged and contrived. But as guesses go, it's an educated one and I'd bet my mellow yellow motor that I'm right. I'd even throw in my old Bowie collection.

Of course, he could drive straight over and recount my desperate plot to undo them and then swear his undying love. He could even go as far as to tell her that not having a child together doesn't really matter anyway. That she's all that matters.

But that's not all that's eating away at Rory as he drives away from here. There's also the certain knowledge that for a year or more the woman he wants to spend the rest of his life with has been lying to him. Worse still, he found this out from the mouth of the very shit he had called on to sort out.

I love it when I'm brilliant. I give myself a wink in the mirror and marvel at how much younger I look than my recently departed visitor.

It never dawned on me before tonight that I could be this malicious and vindictive. But I'm not so much interested in destroying whatever it is Clare and Rory have going for them as I am in trying to salvage something of what we once had ourselves. Pathetic and doomed maybe but I have to try. God has a soft spot for triers.

Truth is though, Clare was been cheating on the both of us, in a way. I found out first and have had nearly a year to try and come to terms with it. I wonder how Rory will cope. Time will tell and it won't take a whole lot of it either.

The bedside phone begins its insistent burring just as I'm about to drift off but instead of answering, I shove my head under the pillow and ignore it. I know who's at the other end, biting her nails and cursing under her breath. Sinead is like that.

I was supposed to ring her this afternoon after I had dropped Jimmy off, except I forgot. Well actually I didn't, I just chose not to. She's been getting predictably possessive in the past fortnight (my little bathroom is completely colonised now, my toothbrush and razor being the only two things in it that belong to me) and this is my way of reclaiming some time and space.

Having been denied the opportunity to pour invective down the line tonight, she'll tear strips off me in some quiet corner of the office tomorrow. I'll pout, grudgingly apologise and then we'll come back here and do some very rude things to each other. Everyone know that humping is much better after a good row. If I was a sex therapist I'd prescribe it for all my patients.

The phone gives up and I let my heavy head take me wherever it chooses to go and before it downloads for the night, it occurs to me that it would be gas if Sinead and Rory somehow met and fell madly and deeply in love. I reckon there are loads of babies in Sinead and Rory would have great fun finding them. A match made in heaven. A fitting final chapter to this whole saga. There might be a book in this yet. A bestseller, I wouldn't wonder.

# 20

## (Dublin – Then)

I can't make up my mind whether or not I like 10cc. Jimmy has always maintained they're crap but then he hates anything that doesn't have a five-minute drum solo stuck into the middle of it, or doesn't give him an opportunity to show off some nifty riffs on his air guitar.

He was famous for those. Especially at Rory Gallagher concerts.

'Rubber Bullets' is being played on a pirate radio station by some jabbering deejay who annoys me by talking over the start of songs and butting in before they end. Worse again he sounds like Goofy when he laughs and he keeps rabbiting on about the wind chill factor in the bay area.

Bay area my arse. Prick with ears.

Clare is still asleep next to me, although when I turned the radio on low earlier she did seem to stir a little. I cuddle up to her bare back and trace a finger down her well-defined spine which runs like a train track from the base of her neck to her bottom. Not a budge. Dead to the world.

She arrived off the half-six at Heuston last night to spend the weekend, having told her folks that she was staying with her lanky friend, who's now a student nurse in the Mater.

159

Or the Meath. Or possibly both simultaneously.

Instead, Clare's travelled up to help me celebrate my nineteenth birthday, which is today, and to sleep with me for the first time.

We had achieved most of it by degrees already, of course, but this is the first time that we'll have gone to bed and woken up together. I thought it was great but then I don't have a whole lot to compare it with and I wasn't being too fussy, just as long as there was a happy ending.

Lying there unable to defrost after a hasty tip-toe to the loo earlier, I'm reminded again of what a bloody fridge I allowed myself get talked into renting.

This became clear last week when an icy draught began to blow down from the frozen Arctic with seasonal malice. The tacky curtains billowed, the windows rattled constantly and the Super-Ser switch stayed jammed at 'Off'.

The only way to stay warm was to go to a public house with draught excluders and hot whiskeys.

But I'm lucky to have it, or so my new flatmate Peter keeps telling me. We started in the bank on the same day and as we hit it off over a few jars that same evening we decided that whoever found a tolerable flat first would give the other first refusal.

This, seemingly, is that tolerable flat.

Getting the cherished posting to the capital in the first place was easier than expected, simply because a third of all branches are in or around Dublin anyway and the demand for provincial placings is such that my request for a job in the big smoke was just what they wanted to hear.

So here I am and here too is Clare, for two nights anyway. She's stretching now and making those grumbling noises that humans sometimes do just before they offer themselves up to another day.

Not that she has anything to grumble about and when I turn my polite cuddle into something more urgent, she turns to me and responds in kind. Her breath is stale and carries traces of that awful wine but I'm sure mine does too. I fumble under the pillow for a condom and she giggles as she remembers how I had to bin two last night before I managed to unfold one properly. I should have read the instructions first.

Like everything else, it's easy when you know how. I know now. Right first time. That's the boy. Like riding a bike.

We've made space for ourselves on the steps leading to the basement in Toners. Clare has wedged her afternoon shopping between her back and the wall and has a pint jammed between her knees as she tries to sort out the loose change that represents the remainder of her life-savings.

'Christ Dan. I've gone through a fortune,' she tells me, as if I hadn't noticed.

We'd spent the guts of the afternoon elbowing our way through hordes of shoppers who all seemed to be going in the opposite direction to us. This was in the relentless pursuit of the prefect Christmas gift for her Mum and Dad. And for the mad twins. Spoilt little wagons.

Whenever I stopped to grumble as another store swallowed us up, I was given one of those smiles of hers. Then she fidgeted with my scarf and went on about how she rarely got to Dublin and how the shops were just fab. They look exactly the same as the shops in Cork to me but there was not much point in saying that. The argument had already been lost and I got a quick peck on the cheek by way of compensation.

It was after five before she gave in and I coaxed her into seeing *Annie Hall* against her better judgement. We argued about it all the way from the Adelphi to the pub afterwards. Clare, it transpires, has a thing about Woody Allen. A hate thing. Unreal. If I coupled this fact with her indifference to David Bowie, I could have doubts about our suitability for each other. I don't dwell on it.

'Have you enough dosh to buy your round?'

'Just about,' she says, 'and a bag of chips on the way home.'

'What more could you want. Anyway, your sugar daddy is a banker now, so you won't do without.'

She flutters her eyelids and clutches her heart in gratitude. I must tell her some time that sarcasm doesn't suit her.

A solemn Sonny Condell is plucking at his guitar while singing one of his tortured compositions from underneath a bush of curly hair. He seems to sing to the microphone rather than just into it. Like it's his real audience. I come to see him whenever I can and I wanted to show him off to Clare.

We both fall silent and listen to his set, more out of tiredness than reverence, but that will do. It seems that Clare is intrigued by his songs anyway, which is just as well. There are only so many omens I could ignore.

We have to gallop to make the last bus, but we do manage to scramble on board and squeeze ourselves between the tightly packed bodies to find a space for ourselves near the rear. It takes us a while to catch our breaths and when we do Clare gets on her tippy-toes to plant a kiss on my cheek.

'I'm having a fabulous time. Really great. Can't believe I have to head home tomorrow.'

She has to shout to be heard but nobody seems to take any notice.

The bus rattles through Ballsbridge, weaving and rolling as last buses always seem to. Instead of offering a reply that I'd have to shout back, I give her my best grin instead.

She's right though. It is hard to believe that she'll be in Cork this time tomorrow night, resuming her role as daddy's little girl, all safely tucked up in bed after telling her folks a web of complex lies about her friend's lovely bedsit in Phibsboro.

I had been anxious about what this weekend might hold. We had sworn enduring love to each other the night before I left Cork but I wasn't sure that either of us could really have meant it. As the train carried me down the tunnel and out of Cork, I wondered if we could keep a relationship going with only snatched weekends and occasional phone calls to sustain it.

I wondered too about what I'd find up in Dublin or whom I might meet. And it crossed my mind that a girl like Clare, for whom flirting is as natural as breathing itself, might find a new toy to play with. Or even decide that there's something cute about poor, afflicted Donny Osmond after all.

But there's been something about this weekend that has reaffirmed my hunch that Clare Fitz really is the business and if I was a gambler I'd put money on us going the distance. Then, you never can tell.

I'm not much into planning and speculating as a rule. I'm more a here-and-now man but I indulge myself, just this once.

Will we, for instance, still be together next year for my twentieth birthday?

My thirtieth?

Fortieth even?

That will be 1997. Science fiction. Orwell's visions will be old hat then and we'll be in Arthur C. Clarke territory instead. Too scary to contemplate. I decide to let it aside.

Clare gives me a nudge.

'Isn't this our stop?'

It is, and we grab our bags and just about make our way to the front of the bus in time.

'A penny for them,' she says as we walk through Blackrock village.

'What?'

'Whatever it was you were day-dreaming about.'

'Oh that. Nonsense really. I was just trying to figure out where you and I would be when I hit forty.'

'Forty? Christ. What brought that on?'

'Drink, I suppose. Or that thing called love.'

'Okay, I'll hazard a guess . . .

'Don't, Clare. Don't bother. It's scary.'

But she's enjoying herself, so she goes on.

'Well, we'll probably gather around the dining-room table and a maid will carry in a cake with forty candles decorating it. Then the gathered staff will applaud and you and the children will blow them out . . . '

'Children? How many?'

'Six. Yes, at least six.'

'Jesus, Clare. Steady on.'

'Well, how many would you like?'

'It's never crossed my mind.'

164

'How many?'

'Two at the most. And I'm not having any until I'm a thirty-year-old geriatric at the very earliest.'

'Any names?'

She's walking backwards two feet or so in front of me, swinging a bag from each arm and having great fun. Thank Christ it's only the drink talking. I don't like kids much because I can remember being a particularly obnoxious one myself.

'Well, something biblical for a boy, anyway,' I say, hoping that if I play along she might grow tired of the game.

'Like?'

'Samuel.'

'Yuch.'

I think for a second.

'Matthew.'

'Done. And a girl?'

'How about Clare Junior or Danielle.' I don't give it much thought.

'No, Dan. Ever since I was a little girl I've always said I'd call a daughter Sally.'

She's quite emphatic.

'Right. Sally it is. Are we done? Can we hurry up and get out of this freezing bloody cold and go to bed.'

'Sex, sex, sex. Do you fellas ever think of anything else?'

'No.' Which isn't true, of course, but I have the hard-won reputation of an entire gender to protect here.

'Well, imagine what it will be like when you really are forty and you can't get a hard-on any more. Or if you do, you won't be able to see it because of your beer belly.'

I'd rather not.

# 21

## (Dublin – Now)

I am a forty-year-old man. If you take 1957 away from 1997 that's what you're left with. I'm much too young to be so old but there is no arguing with mathematics. I might not feel it, but in the eyes of a callous world I am officially middle-aged, past it and a has-been and have been since 3.03 a.m. this morning.

I have been preparing for this day ever since it dawned on me six months ago that it was imminent and there wasn't much that I could do about it. Still, like an expected death in the family, it sends you reeling when it actually happens.

I haven't said a word to anyone, including Sinead, and only those who have known me a long time and can count that far will work it out. Birthday cards from my dear old Mum, Kevin, Sheila and, surprisingly, Jimmy were shoved through my letterbox this morning while a large homemade one, liberally adorned with painstakingly cut-out Liverpool footballers, came a day early from Matt. Tucked inside it was a much smaller one from Clare, depicting a pastoral scene, with her trademark autograph scribbled across it.

I felt guilty for a minute about not telling Sinead but I wasn't up to her clucking about organising a romantic meal in one of those fussy French restaurants that I hate and forking out for another grossly expensive and inappropriate present.

At a time when I'm trying to create a little bit of distance between us it would have been foolish to give her another foothold in my life, another reason to park herself and her overnight bag in my flat and another to delude herself into thinking that we're going to run and run like some hit musical.

Sinead is fun to go out with, even better fun to stay in with, and her timely intervention in my life is not something I'll easily forget. But I've never given her the slightest reason to believe that I'm in any fit state to throw myself into a serious relationship just after parachuting out of the big one and landing a crumpled heap on hard ground. I thank her for picking me up and dusting me off but I'm feeling much better now thanks.

If that makes me a bastard, so be it. And it's not the first time. A couple of weeks ago I told Rory Bogtrotter something that it was in my best interest for him to know and which might reap benefits yet. I've begun to learn the rudimentary skills of survival a tad late at forty but I'm glad to have them at my disposal nonetheless.

Anyway, I could hardly have told Sinead that my fortieth was around the corner and that I had decided to spend it in the company of my estranged wife and son in a Chinese restaurant. But this is how it is.

Matt phoned me last week to organise it. I could hear his mother shouting from either the kitchen or upstairs to make sure that I had nothing else planned but Matt didn't see that as being a serious consideration, so didn't bother to ask.

They're late, of course, and I sip a Miller and grudgingly admit to myself that I'm tilting towards the nervous. But when they eventually breeze in I can see that I have no reason to be. Clare, in a very sixties twinset and with her hair cut tight the way I like it, is in bubbly form and even plants a kiss on my cheek before she sits down. I try not to look too pleased.

Matt makes jokes about my age, which sound like they've been rehearsed in the car on the way over, and then fumbles in his mother's shoulder bag before pulling out a little gift-wrapped parcel.

'This is from Mum and me,' he says handing it over. 'Open it.'

I pretend that I'm excited and tear off the paper to find a Walkman. Very smart and expensive looking. I'm impressed.

'Fantastic. Thanks Matt.'

'Well I bought it but Mum paid for it.'

'For your hill-walking,' Clare tells me, as if she feels she has to explain herself.

'Well thanks to Mum too. Brilliant present.'

Matt beams at both of us in turn and Clare winks at him. It's nice playing happy family.

We order and then have to wait while Matt takes his time and ours to pore over the menu, giving it the sort of attention that we've only ever seen him devote to Premiership league tables. I convince him that he'd love sweet and sour but when his meal arrives he pokes and sniffs it and only gets around to tasting it after sustained bullying from both of us.

'That's what I miss,' he says, 'the two of you nagging me at the same time.'

That puts us in our place, just as he knew it would, and the only sound from our table for a while is that of working cutlery and the welcome intrusion of a smiling waiter who tops up our wine glasses.

'So how is Siobhan?' Clare asks quietly, as if she's inquiring after a mutual friend whom I had just happened to bump into lately. What she's really wants to know, of course, is why I'm not out on a hot date with Patricia The Stripper on tonight of all nights.

'Sinead,' I correct here, knowing that she meant it.

'Oops, sorry.'

'She's fine. And Rory?

'Rory? Oh, he's grand. Great.'

'He owes me two quid,' Matt interrupts, his mouth full of a meal that he had been making faces at only five minutes ago.

'Don't talk with your mouth full,' Clare says, resigned to the fact that he'll ignore her and shovel in another load of fried rice before going on.

'He bet me Arsenal would beat Liverpool in the league and, of course, they didn't. That was three weeks ago and he still hasn't paid up.'

'I'm sure he will.' I feel obliged to defend the bogtrotter's good name, although I can't imagine why. Something to do with adults sticking together, I suppose.

'Huh. He's been avoiding me since. I haven't seen him in a fortnight. Cheapskate.'

'Enough, Matt. Thank you.' Clare is annoyed or maybe just pretending to be.

'Has he been sick?' I try to sound just as nonchalant as Clare had when she asked me about Sinead but my mind is racing to a single conclusion at an illegal speed. Don't even have time to put on my seat belt.

'No,' she says, avoiding my gaze by picking up the wine bottle and examining the label. She did a wine appreciation course once and can be a bit of a bore on the subject.

'But you're still seeing each other?' I don't bother trying to sound indifferent now and she looks at me surprised.

'None of your business, Dan.' she says but she's only letting on to be annoyed. I can tell. Always could.

I might, if I wished, argue that it is my business, considering that Rory gets to see more of my child than I do and happens to have been regularly bunking down in a house that is still costing me a small fortune in blood, sweat and tears every month. Instead I look vaguely hurt. But I'm only letting on as well.

Clare turns away to help Matt choose his dessert from a laminated ice-cream menu. Once he's ordered a chocolate concoction, she ushers him off to the loo. He goes after vigorous protests.

'Anyway,' she says, placing her elbows on the table and looking me straight in the eye, 'what about you and this Sinead person?'

'Well, I'm trying to disentangle myself a bit, to be honest. Fun while it lasted, if you know what I mean.'

'You mean it was just about getting laid?' Direct as ever, she slaps on the mock shock the way Sinead might her make-up.

'Who's not minding her own business now? But yes, I suppose so.'

'Typical, Dan. Bloody typical.'

I drain the last of the bottle into her glass and change the subject.

'Do you remember the first time we celebrated a birthday of mine up here, in nineteen seventy something, when you came up from Cork for the weekend? You were swotting for your Leaving Cert at the time.'

'Yes. Quite well.'

'Well, I remember wondering at the time if we'd still be together at forty and you telling me that I wouldn't be much use to anybody by then. I'd be past it.'

'Did I? The things you remember!'

'I know. And it's as clear as if it was yesterday. It just came back to me today, for some strange reason. Out of the blue. Bizarre.'

'And?'

'Nothing really, except that we've known each other an awful long time, I suppose. That's all.'

'We have,' she says and is thinking about what to say next when Matt returns, dragging at his trousers zip. Can't take him anywhere.

'Can I ask Dad anyway, Mum?'

'Ask him what?'

'About Christmas, of course.'

'No! You know that's out of the question Matt. We're going to Granny's . . . '

'What about Christmas exactly?'

'If you'd stay with us over Christmas, Dad. Please.'

'Look, stop, Matt. I told you already that it's not possible.' Clare is leaning across the table and glaring at him.

The atmosphere has changed and Matt has obviously asked what he was expressly asked not to. But he ignores her stare and continues after a laboured pause and sigh. He's a cheeky sod at times.

'It's less than two weeks away, Dad.'

'But you're going to your granny's, Matt. Your mum has just said so.'

'That's only for two stupid nights. All that way for two stupid nights in boring old Cork.'

Clare manages to keep her voice down, but I can see that this is exactly the sort of melodrama she did not want a role in tonight. She obviously had her own script prepared and she didn't need this bit-player ad libbing. The penny's beginning to drop.

'Matt, Granny is looking forward to it. You know she is.'

The two of them are locked in unblinking eye-contact and speaking in the sort of whispers that always seem to attract the type of attention they're deliberately designed to discourage. I think of giving Matt a ticking off but curiously don't feel that it's my place.

Clare doesn't reply but begs and scolds him all at once with a particularly penetrating look. I've had my share of those in my time.

'Well, after Granny's. Why not then? Dad, you ask her the real reason why you can't come over after Granny's?'

We're getting odd looks. Ears are primed between courses.

'Could someone explain things to this old-timer? Please.'

Clare gets up, balls her napkin and tosses it in on the table. Drama queen. Always was, to be fair.

'You,' she says, pointing at Matt. 'Up. Your coat. We're going.'

'Jesus, Clare. Your wine. Coffee. Don't spoil the night.'

I'm genuinely astonished and it comes out sounding more desperate than I would have wished.

'I'm sorry, Dan. It's not your fault. This time.'

Matt is near to tears and he sullenly pulls himself up, awkwardly dragging his jacket from the back of the chair, nearly toppling it. He knows well enough that there's a time to take his mother on and a time when it's more advisable to do what he's told. He recognises now that this is one of the latter.

'What about my ice-cream?' The fight has gone out of him and he asks this more in hope than expectation.

'You should have thought of that before.'

'Before what, Clare? What is this?'

'Look Dan, I'll phone you in the next few days and we'll talk. I thought we might be able to tonight. Silly of me. Come on, Matt.'

Matt gives me a hurried, limp hug, wishes me a happy birthday and is about to walk after his mother, who is striding purposefully towards the door, when he turns back to me.

'Mum and Rory had a fight. An almighty row. Hours and hours on the phone so they were. But now they've made up and he's coming over when we get back from Cork and Mum says he might be staying. I thought that if you came, he couldn't.'

He blurts it out and looks relieved for having done so.

I can feel myself begin to meltdown from the core out. The China Syndrome. I feel physically sick. I knew I wanted Clare and Matt back but I didn't realise how much until right now. It's come as something of a revelation.

'Oh, I see,' I say after a long silence but I can't bring myself to lift and turn my head to face him. Can't even bring myself to feel anything for him right now.

Funny how it's my ten-year-old who's telling me that it's finally all over. Funny all right but I don't feel like laughing.

I stick a King Edward in my mouth and pat my pockets in a vain search for matches and when I do look up to say goodnight he's already gone, the door swinging gently behind him.

This is what tonight was really all about. It was about telling me that we were really through. Politely, of course, over a few glasses of wine. Matt sitting between us making it hard for me to beg or cry or just flounce out without paying the bill.

Tonight was also about letting me know that she and the bogman were going into business together. Sign up over the door. Clare & Rory plc. Floated on the Stock Exchange. A gilt-edged investment.

So much for my cunning plan. So much for Rory pissing off to the African Missions as a late vocation. So much for my big birthday night out.

I'd feel sorry for myself if I wasn't such a thick.

# 22

# (CORK)

The bastards promised. Scouts honour. I said Clare will have my guts for garters if I turn up hung over and puke-faced and they said sure, no worries.

No worries? I'm sharing the boot of a Fiat Mirafiori with a whiffy kit bag, jump leads and bag of golf clubs. It's pitch black, with only a glimmer of the red tail lights sneaking through to give me something to focus on as the car bounces down bumpy country roads. God only knows where we'll end up.

It's midnight and I'm getting married in the morning. Well, the afternoon really. The afternoon of Saturday 24 July 1983. That is if I ever get out of here. I bang my fists on the dividing panel.

'Let me out you *fuckers*. You're dead Flynn. All of you. Dead.'

I can hear the muffled laughter from the car and Moss shouts that we're almost there. Honest. More laughter.

I bang my head off the jack that's stacked on the driver's side as we clatter into a pothole that felt like a bomb-crater. I catch my shoulder this time.

'*Bastards!*'

Should never have listened to them. Any of them. Nicely marinated, I could have fallen into a taxi after the Vin. Instead I allowed myself be convinced that the night was young.

We were meandering down Patrick Street, taking up the width of the broad footpath between us, when Jimmy initiated the propaganda campaign.

'It's your stag, for Christ sake. You've got to have a major blow-out. You've got to get smashed.'

I gave in timidly in the end, because I felt I ought to and only after extracting a promise from them that the night wouldn't climax with me tied bollock-naked to a lamppost, painted shocking pink. It's been known to happen.

Of course not, they chorused in something close to harmony. Like they had rehearsed it, which they probably had.

I regretted giving them the idea, even though I reckoned that not even Jimmy could get his hands on a tin of matt emulsion at this time of a Saturday morning. At least I didn't think so.

Then it happened. Bastards. I was picked up and tossed, like a sack of coal, into the boot of Moss Barrett's car, which we just happened to be passing.

A couple, arms wrapped around each other and their faces fixed in astonishment, stopped to gape.

'This mon has been tried and convicted by the Irish Republican Army and you whores saw nuttin'.'

Peter's Belfast accent is passable to my untutored ear but I wasn't in a position to see how they reacted. The lads thought it was hilarious.

All I've been told since is that we're heading in the general direction of West Cork to a little pub that stays open all night, or for as long as the mad old dear who runs it feels like pulling pints.

Between bouts of abuse, I plead with them to let me out. But they just laugh louder.

'I'm fucking suffocating in here. I've got asthma. I'm claustrophobic. I could *die*.'

Barrett has stuck on a Police tape and Peter who's travelled down from Dublin for the weekend, Gerry Clifford, Murph and Jimmy have all joined in on 'Message In A Bottle'. I hate Sting. I usen't to but I do now.

Then the car gives a mighty swerve, there's a screeching of brakes, a roar and then the car rights itself. They all dissolve in heaps of laughter and I nurse another crack across my poll. Out of order.

'*Bastards.*' I shout it as loud as I can and the effort, coupled with an hour of being tossed around like a loose penny in a collection box, makes me feel unwell. Very queasy.

'I'm going to throw up,' I tell them but the stereo is belting out 'Roxanne' so loud now that my wailed threat is lost somewhere between the nasal roar of the engine and the vibrating thump-thump of the bass. I have no chance.

I dread to think what they might have in store for me. I can just imagine a fuming Clare arriving down in the arse end of nowhere, carrying her father's hedge clippers to cut me down from some War of Independence monument. I wonder what colour they'll paint me and I grope around the boot again for a tin of paint. There definitely is none. No brush either. Thank Jesus for small mercies.

I concentrate hard to see if she'd see the funny side on her wedding day but I can't pull it off. She was never one for Jimmy and the boys at the best of times and now, with Cork being a place that we only occasionally visit, tolerance or understanding of their quaint and juvenile customs could not be expected.

I'm six years up in Dublin and I've forgotten what a night on the tear with this lot could be like. I had codded myself into believing that the sort of lunacy we used to indulge in was a merely a matter of historical record now. I even imagined that I could control tonight's events. That I would be in charge. Fool.

From what I can make out from back here, Jimmy's in the driving seat. That's something that hasn't changed either. Moss handed him the keys when he couldn't open the driver's door on the third attempt. Not that Jimmy is anywhere near sober. Not even in the same time zone.

If we're stopped by the cops there'll be a lot of explaining to do. Garda O'Dim might be curious to know if the person locked in the boot is there by choice, for instance. Or, he might ask the smart alec in charge of the vehicle what class of tobacco he's smoking. Non-tipped at the very least.

An intervention like that might be my best bet of getting to the church on time but I'm not depending on it.

After one hour and twenty-seven minutes, the car slows to something approaching the legal limit and every fibre of my being can feel the swells and dips of a boreen pass underneath. We stop, doors open and slam. Then the boot opens and a rush of fresh, salty air bundles in.

Five beaming faces stick their heads around the lid to see how I'm getting on and I repeat some of the obscenities that I prepared earlier, haul myself out without any help and dust myself down.

I launch a wild kick at Jimmy's backside but he dodges and concentrates on rolling another weed.

'None of you cunts are coming to my next stag. Shits. One and all.'

More laughter all round and, against my better judgement, I allow myself a smile.

God only know where we are. All I can tell is that we've driven up what is little more than a dirt road to this pub and away to my left and some distance below I can make out the glass-like Atlantic which is floodlit by a moon that seems to have an interrupted view of this side of the world.

The pub, little more than a cottage with a rusting Murphy's sign hanging precariously from above the door, is coming down with people. There's a traditional group circled around the hearth with their heads bowed in concentration as they give it loads of welly.

*Diddly, diddly, diddly dee . . .*

I wouldn't know one trad number from the next. I'm a child of the seventies. Rock 'n' roll for breakfast, dinner and tea. But this is all right. I might even allow myself to have fun here. When in Rome and all that. Or Ballyarsehole, for that matter.

I decide to put the wedding aside for a few hours and make it a night worthy of the day that follows. Seems appropriate and fitting. So I get the drinks in. Then Jimmy gets in some more. I toast the lads and all the piss-ups we've had before and then raise my glass to all the piss-ups yet to come. I even forgive them for fucking me in the boot. For an hour and twenty-seven minutes. Exactly.

I'm in the mood now. Am I what!

I can't sing, but an hour or so later I get up on the bar

and sing anyway. I do 'Be bop a lula'. I know most of the words, although I seem to start somewhere in the middle and work my way back to the top. Nobody notices. Nobody gives a toss. It's the Lennon version from his *Rock 'n' Roll* album, the last great thing he did and sheer genius on vinyl. I love the man. Rot in hell, Chapman. Sick fuck. I give it loads. Then we're all singing together and the fiddles fall into a sullen silence. Then there's more drink. Lots of it.

And more singing still. Any old shite. Rugby songs. Rebel songs. Rock 'n' Roll. And 'I'm Getting Married in the Morning'.

*Ding dong the bells are going to chime . . .*

When I look at my watch again its half-three and we're the last customers left. It looks like the old dear has pulled her last pint.

So we sing alone, until she flings us out into the night.

Then Jimmy gets one of his ideas. One of his bright ones. The sort that, if I was in charge of my mental faculties, I would shake my head at. Happily, I'm not.

'Let's,' he says, 'go for a fucken swim. In the sea.'

'It looks warm from here,' I say. And it does.

We pile into the car. Someone lets the handbrake off and the Fiat creaks, groans and freewheels her way down the dusty path to the beach a few hundred yards away, occasionally brushing aside the wild fuschia hedges which time and nature have allowed to form an overhanging guard of honour.

We're all singing again.

*'Oh I do like to be beside the seaside,/Oh I do like to be beside the sea . . .*

The part of the Atlantic which washes up against our

shores is a cold, mean son-of-a-bitch, even when the sun has been lavishing care and devotion on it like it has this summer.

But I'm the first to strip off anyway. It's my night after all. I throw my clothes on to the saturated sand that has just been washed flat by a retreating tide. I can easily pick out the white foam in the distance as it lazily throws itself up on the shore.

I run in and wade on through until I the water laps my thighs. Then I plunge down and the cold sucks the breath out me. When it allows it back in I scream as loud if I had been castrated without an anaesthetic.

Then I get used to it, dive in again and when I emerge this time I'm half-way to being sober. A quarter anyway. I feel great. Bloody great. But cold. Bloody freezing.

The rest follow, Cliffy being characteristically reluctant. Down to his boxers and skinnier than when he used to be skinny, he tiptoes around the edge until Peter and Jimmy gather him up, face him southwest and fling him in the general direction of Cuba.

'Jesuuuuuuuuuuuuuuuuuus . . . '

Serves the little bollox right. He was laughing the loudest from the cockpit while I was in an uncomfortable foetal fold in the boot. And if he didn't deserve it for that, it was long overdue for his drunken intervention that night years ago when I got that hiding. So much for forgiving and forgetting.

God only knows why I'm stagging with these guys. Peter's a good drinking mate, my best in Dublin. And Jimmy's Jimmy. But I never see the other lads. I'm acknowledging and honouring the old days, I suppose. Pretending that Cork is still important to me after six years away. It's not really, but at times like this you do what's expected because it's easier. And it was easier to have a stag than not.

A shiver runs through me, the sort that my mother would interpret as someone walking over my grave. But it's simpler than that. It's hypothermia. I can feel myself go numb.

Moss digs out a bottle of Paddy from the glove compartment and we take turns at swallowing generous medicinal mouthfuls in the relative warmth of the car. The engine is revving and Moss keeps telling us that the heater will kick in soon.

Not that anyone has complained. There's just a lot of chattering and muttering but nothing that approaches an intelligible sound. Everybody's too busy trying to get back into clothes that are damp and sand-infested in a very confined space.

Peter sticks his backside in my face as he attempts to pull up his trousers and I have a feeling that when I have cause to remember my stag in years to come that this might well be the image that escapes from my memory. Hairy bastard. Unnatural.

The car is reluctant to pull the six of us up a hill that it had so efficiently freewheeled us down. Moss, back in the driving seat now, coaxes it yard by yard. He suggests that someone gets out until we reach the brow but we tell him to piss off in the sort of harmony that was sadly lacking in the pub.

We get there at the very same moment that the sun, a blazing dome of brilliant white, is edging its way over a wedge of mountains to our right.

'It's going to be a scorcher,' Peter says, 'a fucking scorcher.'

We all stare at it for a few seconds. It's not very often that any of us would get to see a sunrise. Not one as majestic as this one, anyway.

Jimmy throws an arm over my shoulder and then pats me on the back of the head.

'It's certainly going to be a scorcher for this poor bastard, anyway,' he says and there's a big cheer and Moss presses the horn, scattering an assembly of curious sheep up a rocky hillside.

'What time is it?' I try to sound indifferent and the yawn that goes with the question is not for effect.

'Five to five.'

'Get me home for fuck sake. I've got to get some kip.'

Jimmy does his Lennon thing, starting into 'The Ballad of John and Yoko'. Sounds just like him too. Pure Scouse.

We negotiate our way back to the main road and someone rolls one and each of us gets a drags in strict rotation. I'm allowed an especially long one because of the day that's in it.

Someone else puts on 'Blood on the Tracks' and everyone grows quiet and everything turns mellow.

When the decision was made a few miles outside the city to head to an early house I was asleep. Snoring, seemingly, my head jammed up against a side window, my cheek Superglued to it. Murph said I must have looked like the victim of a Mafia hit from the outside. But I don't think I could have looked that good.

Someone shook me awake and we spilled, bedraggled, half-dressed and fully cut into a docker's pub somewhere off Victoria Road. That's when I remembered that I had left my runners behind on the strand. Good ones too. Adidas. Bought them for the honeymoon.

I allowed myself to be ushered to a seat under a telly that was showing golf highlights from some sunny, green place. Greg Norman was on the tee box. The hat. I'd know that hat anywhere. Pissed or otherwise.

The place was next to empty, except for two hardy-looking old-timers stooped over the bar in a conspiratorial conversation. One of them had a bookie's docket in his hand and they were trying to make out the writing.

Jimmy bought me a pint, stuck a half-smoked cigarette in my mouth, slapped me across the face and kissed me on the forehead. The Bass clock above the bar read seven-thirty and I swore to myself that I'd phone a taxi at eight.

Then when I looked again the small hand had managed to find its way right up to ten and nobody had bothered to tell me. Mostly I think because the lads were only vaguely conscious of what day it was and had totally given up on hours.

That's how I explained it to Clare at lunchtime over the phone anyway. She wasn't too pleased. I had been given a list of things to do this morning. Flowers and place settings and the like. Totally forgot.

'Should have known. Whenever Jimmy Flynn is around. I should have known. Are you still drunk?'

'Don't be ridiculous. I'll just get a few hours' kip and I'll be fine.'

'A few hours' kip? We're supposed to be getting married in two hours' time, Dan. *Remember*? Christ.'

She was trying to keep a lid on her voice and only just managing to. Her mother was probably earwigging. I mumbled an apology and swore that everything was okey-doke and she just about resisted the temptation to bang the phone down.

Instead she muttered something about not making a show of her today.

I'd have felt guilty if I had the energy for such a luxury. But what reserves I did have would have to be rationed out carefully over the long day ahead.

Chastened, I ran myself a hot, deep Radox bath and submerged myself in it, knowing that when I climbed back out that the mother would have everything ready, down to the neatly folded and ironed handkerchief. I nodded off in the steaming water and only the gathering of bubbles around my nostrils brought me back to my delicate senses.

I'm feeling human now, although the temptation to collapse on to the bed and crash is almost an irresistible one. But it's not an option. Not if I want to live to see another sunrise.

My mother, her face florid from a morning of vintage fussing, knocks on the bedroom door and asks if I'm decent. It must be the handkerchief. It is.

I give her a big hug but she doesn't reciprocate with the sort of enthusiasm that a youngest son deserves on his wedding day. Then, as if taking offence at something, she withdraws smartly.

'My God. The smell of drink. And what's that's in your hair. Sand? How in the name of all that's holy? Oh don't tell me.' She waves an arm in the air.

I give my head a shake and, sure enough, more of the silvery stuff drifts down to my shoulders. After a bath and all.

'It's nothing. Honest Mum.'

'I would have thought that at twenty-six you'd be beyond this sort of carry on. Treat a smart girl like Clare like that and she'll show you the door. And no mistake.'

I know what's next on the agenda of the meeting. It's been a while since I've heard it, but I'd recognise it coming from any distance.

She sighs before continuing.

'But then you always had to be different to the others. Never any bother. Either of them. I don't remember Kevin falling in the door a few hours before his wedding smelling like Murphy's brewery.'

I say nothing and retreat back upstairs to look for my dickie bow. I could tell her how Kevin had gone off and got himself laid on his stag night. His mates fixed him up with a brasser. Oriental bird, if you please. Told me himself after one too many.

So there.

The very same Kevin has arrived downstairs and I can hear my mother drone on about how Dan never lost it, never grew up and never will. I can't hear the words from up here but I don't have to. He'll be putting his eyes up to heaven around now for her benefit. Shifty hypocrite. My best man but a shifty hypocrite nonetheless.

I look in the mirror, push back my shoulders, flatten down my hair and give myself a wink and a smile. I don't look half bad. Handsome, in a word. This Clare Fitz is a lucky girl.

I cup my hands over my mouth and test my breath for alcoholic purity. It's the only giveaway really. I can live with that and circumstances will overtake it anyway.

Kevin shouts up the stairs.

'Come on little brother, it's execution time.'

I take a deep breathe and tell myself that I'm about to get married. I say the words out loud to myself to see if they'll register. They do and it's a sobering thought.

Considering my delicate state, a sobering thought is just what I need.

*Ding dong the bells are going to chime . . .*

# 23

## (DUBLIN)

I can hear Matt give cheek and I smile to myself. The same cheek that I used to get from him every Saturday morning.

'But I never get my game, so why should I bother to turn up for training.'

I can make him out through the frosted glass in the porch. He's sorting out his gear and I can hear him plainly. His mother, her voice trailing down from somewhere upstairs, is indistinct, but I know what she's telling him anyway.

'Just go, Matt. Now.'

I wait for this little weekend ritual to play itself out before I ring the bell. Not that I should be here at all.

Normally, I pick up Matt after lunch on Saturday and return him, spick and span and spoilt, around teatime Sunday. It's not a formal arrangement. It hasn't had to be. So far.

Instead I should be in Cork. Kevin and Sheila had arranged a meal out with Mum to celebrate my birthday but after that fiasco with Clare and Matt the other night I didn't have the stomach for it. Couldn't face the drive. Couldn't face them.

I rang Kevin on Thursday and told him I had a touch of the flu and wouldn't be able to make it. I don't think he believed me. Something in my voice, I suspect. To lie properly you really have to work at it and my heart wasn't in it. It's not in anything.

We've been apart four months but it was only over that Chinese the other night that the finality of it all struck me. As I drove home it clicked that I had been playing games all along without even knowing it. Silly games. Games in which I made up the rules as I went along. Like the time I walked out. Like the way I manipulated Sinead. Like my master plan to airbrush Rory out of the picture.

But just because you invent a game doesn't necessarily mean you're any good at it. A bit like the English and tennis.

The last two days at work have been difficult. Nothing to do with the actual work. These days I just keep my head down, furrow my brow, chew on my Bic and looked like I'm part of the team. That way Danaher might stay away. And that's my only remaining career ambition. Keeping Danaher at arm's length.

The difficult part has been trying to avoid Sinead. I couldn't bear one of her inquisitions now, or have the mental agility to make up another convincing excuse why any night in the foreseeable future would be a bad night for her to drop by the flat.

I did notice that she sighed herself into a sulk when I told her I wasn't going to the pub yesterday. Suit yourself, she said, and walked off. I didn't read much into it at the time. I wasn't taking too much notice. But maybe the penny's finally dropped. Ping. Smart girl, Sinead. I might even get my bathroom back one of these days.

'Hiya.'

'Dad. Didn't expect to see you today!'

He sticks his head back around the door.

'Mum. It's Dad.'

'Shouldn't you be at training by now?'

'I'm just going.'

'Never play for Liverpool if you're late for training . . . '

He has a quick look at his watch, pulls a face and he's gone.

Clare meets me in the hall, a look of puzzlement on her face and the top of her wine dressing-gown bunched in her fist for the sake of modesty. As if I were a stranger. Or an unannounced Jehovah's Witness who's come to barter for her soul.

'Aren't you supposed to be in Cork? Wasn't that this weekend?'

'Ah, I wasn't up to it.'

'Oh?'

I pause, stroll past her uninvited to the kitchen and sit down, my hands buried deep in my jacket pockets. It's cold in here. The heating hasn't been put on. Typical Clare. Totally scattered around the house. Totally focused everywhere else.

She fusses with the breadboard, tilting a scattering of brown soda crumbs into the pedalbin. Clare always has brown soda and freshly squeezed orange juice for breakfast. Day in and day out.

She asks me if I'd fancy a cup of tea.

'Please.'

'So have you come for Matt or something?'

'No.'

'What then?'

'Well you said you'd ring. Explain. You know. That scene with Matt.'

She turns to face me, searching my face to see what it is exactly that I need to know. I look out the window to a garden that has been abandoned to the winter.

I don't need to know anything, of course. It was spelt out to me quite clearly and succinctly by Matt. But I want to hear it from Clare's lips this time. I want her to make it official. I want her to tell me to my face that our marriage is a corpse. A stiff. Laid out on a slab in a cold morgue. I'm here to identify the body. For the state records.

But Clare is hedging. She could do without this of a Saturday morning. Her favourite few hours of the week. It always has been.

'It's just that he shouldn't have asked you over for Christmas because we're going to Cork until the 27th. That's the Saturday.'

'And after that?' I sound insistent, which is good.

'I think Matt may have told you.'

There's a trace of irritation in her voice. She unties her robe so that she can redo it properly, briefly revealing a skimpy satin nightie which I don't recognise. All she ever seemed to wear when we shared a bed was the sensible sort Doris Day wore in those movies. Just the sort of contraceptive the Church of Rome used to approve of – and still does.

'Rory is coming here. For the New Year. And possibly beyond. Or so Matt tells me. Is that right?' Even more insistent.

She turns her back again, waiting for the kettle to boil. But watched kettles never do and the silence is a damning one. A denial would have only taken a second. Less.

When Clare does speak, that trace of agitation is replaced by an air of defiance.

'Yes Dan, Rory will be here for the New Year. And yes, it's true too that if it works out – if it works out for Matt that is – he might not be leaving.'

No hedging there. It's official. All the relevant papers signed. Corpse identified. That's my marriage laid out over there all right.

Clare turns away to get down the caddy of tea bags. A timely distraction.

'But I thought you two had run out of steam. I thought even that we might be able to work something out. Not immediately, or anything, but in time.'

She's looking at me now, all right. There's a look of incredulity on her face that she makes no attempt to mask.

'Did you really? And did you honestly think that you'd split us up by telling Rory that we couldn't have children'?

I'd rather not answer that. I plead the Fifth with a shrug and wait for her to continue.

'And even if Rory and me did pack it in, what makes you think that we could ever make a go of it again?'

I think for a while, shifting in my seat and toying with a table mat. Then I just shrug my shoulders again like a little boy who's run out of tall stories and excuses.

'Dunno, to be honest.'

And I don't. To be honest.

'Look, Dan . . . '

She hesitates, chewing over her thoughts for a second longer. 'I've thought this out as best I can. I think, in the long run, it's best for Matt too. All of us really.'

It's the way she says it that gets to me. All nice and caring. I can handle her being the hard bitch. But not this.

I can feel myself fill up and my face turn hot. Prickly.

Overcome, like a mourner at a funeral who's been putting on a brave face, I bury my hands in my face and start to sob. Big, heaving, liquid sobs.

I don't want to. Don't mean to. But I do. Shit.

I can feel Clare's hand resting lightly on my quivering shoulder, more hovering really. Not enough to give consolation but enough to let me know that she's not totally heartless.

I fumble in my pockets for tissues and try to compose myself.

'So are we talking divorce and all that crap, Clare?' My words are wobbly, the tone bordering on the pathetic.

'I haven't thought that far ahead, Dan,' she says and when I look up I can see that she's totally composed and unmoved.

'I'll take that as a yes,' I say, angry now. Angry that I'm bordering on the incoherent at a time when a bit of resolve and restraint would have won more brownie points. Angry too that she really couldn't give a continental.

I get up abruptly before she has a chance to move away. We're standing closer than we've been for a very long time. I can smell her. She hasn't showered yet. That vague hint of perfume, that lingering smell of sleep. I look at her, trying to trap her eyes with mine but she's not having any of it. Angry a moment ago, I'm putty now.

My left hand gently tugs at the tie of her robe and it falls open. She doesn't move, just seems frozen to the spot. I put my hand on her waist and run it quickly up to her breast and let it rest there. That nipple. Almost unfamiliar now but not quite.

Anger flashing across her face, she grabs my wrist and roughly pushes my hand away and backs off.

'Don't you dare.'

There's a light tremor in there among all that venom but her look is not open to interpretation. It's one of plain and simple contempt.

'Get out.'

It's little more than a whisper but she spits it at me. Standing well away now, she avoids my eyes again and shivers.

'There's no need to make a drama out of it. Jesus, Clare. I just . . . '

'Shut up. As if I'd do anything with you. Get out.'

'Is it really that horrible? When I touch you? Do you really hate me that much?'

I'm shouting.

'Yes it is and yes I do. Now fuck off!'

She's shouting too.

I wait for Matt on the edge of the green, the Beetle idling and Crowded House blaring so loud that it bounces off the doors and windows and drowns out my thoughts.

I beep when I see him and he comes smiling and running towards the car, dragging his gear so low that it bounces off the ground.

'Hiya, Dad.' He leaps in, lobbing the bag into the back seat.

'Thought you'd never finish. Hungry?'

'Ya. Famished and thirsty. Scored in training. In off the post. There's only one Jamie Redknapp . . . '

'Well done.'

I drive off, calm now that Matt's here. In control again, although I can tell that my colour is still high by the heat on my cheeks. Matt doesn't notice.

'Where are we going?

'How about a McDonald's? In Bray. It's closest.'

'Brill. But Mum told me to go straight home. Something to do with last-minute Christmas shopping.' He rolls his eyes as children do when they have to explain the things adults waste their time on.

'Don't worry about that.'

He shrugs, so I know he won't.

He devours his Big Mac. I just swirl indifferent coffee around a cup as he yaps incessantly about Liverpool. It's as if the other night had never happened. I nod, open my eyes in wide surprise at suitable intervals and wonder how to get around to the only thing on my mind.

Afterwards we take a stroll on the prom. The sea is ship-grey, faithfully reflecting the heavy clouds that are hanging around looking for trouble. We stop, lean on the old railings and watch the sluggish waves wrap themselves around the steps and then reluctantly withdraw before rising up again.

I catch Matt looking at me and I can tell that he has something on his mind other than football after all.

'Do you hate Mum now, Dad?'

I wasn't expecting that.

'Me? Hate your mum? No. 'Course not.'

'Even though she won't have you back?'

I shrug, look skywards and catch a big drop of rain on my forehead. He's obviously been briefed.

'We'd better get indoors. It's going to pour.'

He ignores me and goes on.

'And even though Rory is moving in?'

'It doesn't matter what I think, Matt. It's how you feel

that matters; you're the important one.'

'Oh, am I? Didn't notice.'

It's raining properly now but neither of us really cares.

'Look Matt. It's one of those things. It's nobody's fault really.'

'Oh yes it is.'

'Whose, then?'

'Yours. Mostly.'

He looks at me, his eyes fill up and he walks into the rain and towards the car.

'Wait, Matt. Let's go the pub and we'll have a chat.'

'I don't want to have a chat.'

'All right. We won't. Just have a Coke or something.'

'No. Just had one. I want to go home. If you won't take me I'll walk.'

I drape my arm over his shoulder, gently drag him back and tell him everything will be fine. He doesn't say anything because he knows it's not true and because he's sealed his mouth shut in an effort to keep the crying inside.

Rory's car is in the drive when we get back, bunched up against Clare's to keep the pavement clear. Alerted by the trademark throaty whine of the Beetle, Clare charges out the front door, marches right up to the car and raps at the window with her knuckleduster of a ring. It had been her great aunt's or something. Hideous-looking thing. I used to make her take it off before we made love.

I take my time in winding it down and watch her get madder. And wetter. Matt hasn't budged.

'Where did you take him?'

'Take him?'

'Yes, take him. You had no right.'

'We just went to McDonald's, Mum.'

'He's my son. I'll take him where I please, when I please.'

'You had no right, you shit. None. I was scared stiff. He was due home over two hours ago.'

'Jesus Christ. I don't believe this. Did you think I was going to drag him off to Iran and raise him as a shagging Muslim?'

We're yelling again and if it wasn't for the rain pelting noisily down, the whole estate would be in on it.

'Get in home, Matt. I told you I had to go shopping. You knew.'

Matt drags his kit from the back seat and leaves wordlessly, not bothering to exercise his alibi or even acknowledge my goodbye. I rev the engine and Clare takes a step back but makes no move to go inside. She has something else to say and I'm curious to find out what it is.

'Well. Can I go now?'

She points a finger at me and takes a step forward again. She's fit to be tied. Lucky old Rory.

'You helped me make up my mind about a few things today, Daniel Hayes. You really did. All those lingering doubts that were nagging away at me. The little niggling pangs of guilt. They're all gone now. I should be grateful really.'

'Just because I bought my son a bag of chips?'

'You know damn well, you bastard.'

'Oh, that. Well, I just thought that after a year of having it away with a sweaty smallholder that you might like to shag someone who showers occasionally. My mistake. Sorry.'

I shouldn't have said that. Thought it maybe but not said

it. Still, I smile, declutch and make to slide the car gently off the pavement when Clare grabs the side mirror and drags and pulls at it with both hands until it snaps right off at the wing. It makes a horrible sound when it does.

I brake and sit there speechless. Clare looks at her trophy, turning it over in her hands a few times as if wondering how it got there, before lobbing the thing in the window on to my lap. I look at it and see myself looking back. I look suitably gobsmacked.

She's half-way up the drive when I think of something to say and it's not particularly brilliant. But at least I sound calm, even though I have to roar it.

'I'll send you the bill, Clare.'

Rory is standing in the porch now, looking like he might after discovering a bit of mischief at the back of his class. I suppose it's his menacing pose. Best to ignore him. Dipstick.

Clare turns and takes a few steps towards the car again. Arms tightly folded.

'No. That's not how it works, Dan, I'm afraid. It's the stupid sod of a husband who gets all the bills.'

Soaked through, with her hair clinging to her scalp and her jeans stuck to her thighs, Clare looks almost triumphant now. As if this was a battle that she had been waiting to fight and now it was fought and won. She's even had the last word. That's how she looks anyway.

She turns her back for the final time and walks towards the front door. Our front door. I paid for it too. Varnished it. Screwed on the brass number on a wet Saturday just like this one.

When I look in the rearview mirror I can just about make out Clare and Rory embrace. Maybe my eyes are playing tricks in the rain. Very indiscreet if they are. As if we hadn't put on enough of a show for the neighbours already.

Not that it matters to me. They're not my neighbours any more. And never will be again. I know that now.

# 24

## (Cork)

I crash on to the bed, shut my eyes and find myself drifting off. Thank God that's over. What a strain. That speech. That first dance. My mother. Her mother. Especially her mother. Wicked Witch of the South.

The first thing Clare did when we escaped to our room was untangle herself from that bloody wedding dress, fling it into a corner and make for the bathroom. She's pie-eyed but not in such a way that any of her starchy old aunts would have noticed. Clare can carry it off, except that she gets a bit giggly. She's singing in the shower, but I can't make out exactly what, although it sounds like the 'Birdie Song'. I'd smile if I could, but the body is shutting down. I haven't slept for two days and even if I wanted to stay awake my body wouldn't be up to it.

I didn't drink too much. All I had to do really was keep last night's dosage on modest top-up. But I did have a discreet joint in the loo before the meal and another immediately after. Jimmy fixed that with a nod and a wink. To keep me calm he said. In case I got wired.

The sequence of events seems to have become jumbled after that and I'd have trouble putting them into anything resembling chronological order.

Kevin's speech wasn't as good as he thought it was but Mum liked it. He couldn't resist mentioning that infamous occasion when I was chased out of school by a teacher, the very afternoon of my first date with herself.

Or how angel-of-mercy Clare visited me when I was a heap of broken bones in hospital and helped me to a miraculous recovery.

Aw.

' . . . and they've never looked back.'

Cheers and hoots and a few wisecracks from the cheap seats.

Kevin even slipped in a reference to last night's stag, telling those guests who didn't already know that if I had turned up any later I'd have missed the starter. Hilarious.

This earned me a withering down-table glare from Clare's mother. I pretended not to notice and looked right through her to my father-in-law a few places beyond and winked. He raised his glass and smiled. Nice man.

The bitch could at least have pretended to be enjoying herself. If only for the day and if only for her daughter's sake. She could have gone back to despising her son-in-law, the bank clerk, tomorrow. Instead she picked at her food and delicately dabbed the corner of her mouth with a serviette, like she was the bloody Queen Mother or some-body.

After the meal I lost track of her. Maybe she choked on a turkey bone and slipped under the table unnoticed. I'd gladly chip in for the cremation. I remember dancing with Clare's Scottish aunt somewhere in there too. An enormous women in a floral dress, she waltzed me around the maple floor and I don't think my feet touched the ground once. Later she crushed me in one almighty hug and said we must visit her in Dumbarton some time.

Or was it Dunfermline?

Then there was Jimmy on electric guitar. He got the band to back him and he went ape.

> *Come a little closer huh, ah will ya, huh,*
> *Close enough to look in my eyes Sharona*

It brought the house down and my ma gave him a big wet kiss. He was nearly mortified.

Clare's father got up to sing 'Danny Boy' and dropped the microphone because he was, as he put it himself, a bit tipsy. Only he'd say that. The feedback bounced off the walls and he couldn't stop apologising. The Wicked Witch won't have approved. Poor man will get it going home in the car.

Someone mentioned that the twins, feeling as awkward as they looked in their flouncy bridesmaid dresses, got up to something as well, but for the life of me I can't remember what exactly. Something to do with Drink and Sick. They'll get it going home in the car too.

The rest will come to me in time and even if it doesn't I'll be reminded of it often enough. Weddings are like that and wedding albums were invented in case you ever tried to forget.

The bed bounces and Clare is sitting on top of me, a bath towel loosely draped around her waist. Her hair is dripping wet and she shakes her head, showering me with cold drops. If a dog did that I'd turf it out.

'Wake up. Christ, it's our wedding night.'

I gather up my scattered senses, or at least as many as I can find at such short notice and run my hands along her thighs. They're warm and wet.

'Come on, Daniel. Sex. Lots of it. I'm drunk and horny and I want to see if it's still fun when it's not a sin.'

She undoes the fly of my rented tux, leaps off the bed and pulls down my trousers. Throwing away her towel, she climbs back on top giggling.

'What's this?'

She rubs traces of sand between her fingers.

' Jesus. What exactly were you up to last night?'

'Oh that. The lads chipped in and got me a mermaid and the two of us had it away in the sand dunes.'

'That must have been nice. What was she like?'

'Slippery. And moist. Very, very moist.'

She laughs, gives me a slap and starts to drag off the rest of my clothes. Properly awake now, I'm as eager as my condition allows. Which isn't very.

'It has to be loud, Dan. Very loud. I want to be embarrassed going down for breakfast in the morning. It's traditional. Bags on top.'

It's how she likes it and tonight that suits me fine.

Afterwards she falls off in a heap and goes asleep with indecent haste, muttering before she does about how much she loves me and wasn't it a great fucking day.

I say it was, tell her I love her too and pull a sheet up to her shoulder. Then I click off the headboard light and tuck myself in close.

The last thing I tell myself is that I'm a lucky bastard. The last thing I hear is Jimmy echoing in the back of my head.

*Is it just ddddestiny, destiny*
*Or is it just a game in my mind Sharona.*

# 25

## (Dublin)

Eoin Kavanagh is the official office bore and it appears that I'm his victim tonight. He has me corralled in an alcove of the pub and is earnestly telling me how it's high time we saw things from the Unionist perspective.

I nod, sip, stifle a yawn and keep my eyes trained over his left shoulder where I can get a good view of the door. She hasn't turned up yet, although I know she will.

'You see, we have to remember that they've come through a quarter of a century of Provo genocide.'

'Bastards.'

'The Unionists?'

'No. The Provos.'

He nods, relieved. A like mind. This encourages him to expand his argument. Revisionism he calls it. A load of boring bollox more like. One lot up there deserves the other as far as I'm concerned. I just felt obliged to say something and it was simpler to say something agreeable.

The branch broke up for Christmas this afternoon and we've moved *en masse* across the road to the pub. It's usually a bit of a blow-out and I could do with one of those. After that business with Clare last weekend it's the least I deserve. It's the least I need.

Not that the intervening week has been dry or anything remotely like it. But my drinking has been of the solitary kind, a brimming glass of Jameson in one hand and the remote control in the other. In the end it just made me more depressed and morbid.

Tonight I'm going to try and forget about the whole mess for a while and get nicely soaked. I have hopes of making it up to Sinead too. I've been mean to her and she didn't deserve any of it. I've bought her a pretty, gift-wrapped necklace in Weirs and I'm keeping my fingers crossed.

She had been smothering me at a time when my life was in a state of flux. It's not in a state of flux any more. Not that kind of flux anyway. At least I know where I stand now. Right now I need smothering. I need someone in my flat, in my bathroom, in my bed.

Cynical maybe but I'm doing what I need to survive. Doing what's best. Best for me at any rate. I'm all I have left.

'And Article Two and Three have to go. That Constitution of ours is half the problem, you know.'

No I don't know but I nod again and allow my eyes light up as if I was beginning to understand the Troubles for the first time. Then the door swings open again and this time Sinead walks in. She's wearing a new dress, or at least one I've never seen before. It's black, skimpy and very Sinead. Heads swivel, but then they always do.

'Drink, Eoin?'

I point at his empty glass, which he has been using as a prop during the whole tutorial.

'No. I'm driving.' He looks at his watch. 'Better be off actually.'

Thank God for that. We exchange seasonal greetings and I head for the bar to buy myself a drink. A stiff one this time. Pints are wasted on me these days.

I eventually catch her eye and raise my glass to her.

'Happy Christmas, Sinead.'

I lean across and give her a peck on the cheek. She's decidedly cool but excuses herself from the cluster of colleagues she's been talking to and comes over to me. It's the quiet end of the bar and we won't be overheard.

'To what do I owe this honour, Dan?'

'Honour. What honour?'

'You being civil to me. I'd forgotten what it was like.'

There's a touch of steel in her voice, the sort of steel that she normally keeps for particularly unreasonable customers. And Spanish students cashing their travellers cheques. She hates them.

'You're right. I'm sorry. It's been a difficult time for me. It still is.'

She leans closer and I can tell from her expression that she isn't about to sympathise. There's steel in her eyes too.

'So that gives you the right to dump me, treat me like shit in front of the whole office? Does it?'

This isn't what I expected. I can't think of anything to say and tinkle the ice in my glass instead. I could say I didn't dump her but she already knows better. At least nobody near has noticed, although you can never tell.

'You used me, Dan. And I was a right fool not to see it coming.'

This has taken me by surprise. I try to think on my feet.

'Look, let's get out of here, have a bite and a proper talk . . . '

'No. There's nothing to talk about.'

Canavan sneaks a look over the rim of his pint glass and when I catch him he looks away, his neck reddening. Others must be eavesdropping too and confirming to their satisfaction what they had guessed long ago. That Hayes has been getting the leg over. Dirty dog. Woof, woof.

'Fair enough.'

'And another thing, while we're at it. Why didn't you tell me about your birthday?'

So that's it. God only knows how she found out but it doesn't matter now.

'Well, Dan?'

'Didn't think it was important.'

'Liar. You wanted to be rid of me. Well, now you are. You must be pleased.'

She picks up her glass and turns to go. I put my hand gently on hers.

'Please. Please. Sinead. Listen.'

She rolls her eyes, but stands still.

'I'm listening.'

Time isn't on my side so I cut to the chase.

'I need you Sinead. Honestly. Really badly.'

'Oh right. Man dumps wife; shags office bimbo; misses home; dumps bimbo; wife says piss off; wants to shag bimbo again.'

That must be how it looks to her and any independent government inquiry would find in her favour, the file going swiftly to the DPP. But there's more to it than that. There's more to me than that. I think so anyway.

Desperate, I root in my pocket for her present. This isn't how I imagined it. I thought maybe over a late Italian. Or in bed. Just before. Just after. In between. During.

She sees it coming.

'No Dan. No. Thanks, but no thanks. No way.'

She pushes my hand firmly back into my pocket and I can see that she means it. Her face is set hard, even if her eyes have ditched the steel and defaulted to hurt. I've blown it.

'I'm getting too old to be making a fool of myself like this, Dan. I suppose I should be grateful for the lesson you taught me.'

I turn from her, lean on the counter and stare straight ahead. This she takes as a sign of abject surrender. She gently lays a hand on my arm.

'Happy Christmas, Dan,' she says only a shade sarcastically, 'and a belated happy birthday. How old?'

'Forty,' I say without turning, surprised that she didn't know and then realising that I don't know her age either.

'Forty? I had you down for thirty-seven. Maybe eight. You don't look it.'

I could say that I feel it, but it would be a waste of breath. I save it for ordering a double Jameson.


We end up in an Indian. The same one I went to with Sinead that first night. That doesn't dawn on me for a while, because I'm very drunk. So drunk that Canavan offered to order me a taxi home when we left the pub. I declined politely. At least I think I was polite.

There's twenty of us or so crammed into a small private room upstairs and Sinead is sitting opposite and a few places down at the same table. She's nice when she has to be but has avoided my company as much as possible all evening. I think she only came to the restaurant because she thought I had been put in a taxi home. Tough.

She's in deep conversation with Willie Roche, a cocky young bastard who ties his hair back in a ponytail, a fashion statement which is still considered bold in the stodgy world of the bank. He wears an earring at weekends too. He told me this in the canteen one day and I think I was supposed to be impressed.

Behind this carefully nurtured image and the well-modulated south-county accent lurks just another pliable twenty-something anxious to get on and desperate to please. The eighties and nineties have produced his sort in spades. They're the Duran Duran generation. The sort of little shits who'd live in Danaher's underwear if there was room.

And he can't hold his drink. None of them can.

Sinead keeps blowing smoke in his face, which he seems to regard as some sort of mating signal. In return he leans forward, whispers something into her ear and she throws her head back laughing. This is all for my benefit. I know it is. She's using the poor sap.

I turn the other way and make an effort to involve myself in other conversations but I'm too far gone to catch up with any of them and too blitzed to initiate any of my own. I admit defeat, claim a bottle of the house red as my own and converse with that instead. We get on famously.

When I look their way again I see Roche get up and head to the loo, a Hamlet stuck in his pretty face and his shirt tail sticking out. I stand up, wobble, sit down and try again. Then I follow him.

I don't mean to say anything. It just comes out. I'm not certain what it is I say, other than it is something along the lines of him being a little toe rag who was out of his depth with a class act like Sinead.

He prods me with a bony finger and says it's none of my fucking business and that my marriage wouldn't be such a shambles if I didn't spend my time screwing around.

Out of order. Drink or no drink. Cheeky cunt.

It is only a shove but he slips on the urinal and goes down heavily on his arse.

'Oh Christ!'

He moans a bit, curses loudly and frantically swaps piss from his hands to his trousers.

I leave him there and I am almost back to my chair when I hear Sinead yell.

'Jesus. Willie. Don't.'

But he does.

He jumps on me from behind and his momentum propels us both across the room until we crash to the floor. We roll over, take a table, everything on it, and a couple of chairs with us. There's uproar and before we have a chance to disentangle limbs we're dragged to our feet and pulled apart.

The owner has gone berserk, his fists clutching at the tufts of hair on the margins of his balding head. Sitcom stuff.

'Out. Out. All out. I call the police this moment. Out, the damn lot of you.'

Danaher takes him aside, drapes an arm over the distraught man's shoulder and tries to calm him down. Then glares at me and Roche in turn.

'For Christ sake, lads.'

I've about caught my breathe now and I allow time for my anger to subside. Roche shrugs off his minders, grabs his coat from the back of the chair and without a glance at Sinead, who's crying quietly to herself, he storms out.

'What a wanker,' I tell everyone within earshot but all I get are odd looks. I sit down heavily and remember how drunk I am. I feel ill.

Danaher is standing over me, fidgeting with his tie and thinking that he should say something but not sure what. I've never seen him stuck for words before.

I'm not stuck for words at all.

'Look. This is outside your jurisdiction, Danaher. Fuck off and mind your own poxy business.'

That causes a ripple all right. I've made their night. The best Christmas piss-up ever.

I haul myself up, the eyes of the still room on me, and walk slowly around the table to where Sinead is no longer crying but pulling desperately on a cigarette. She's wishing the world would end this instant, all records of our civilisation obliterated with it. Or maybe she's just praying that I go away.

'I'm sorry,' I say quietly, and forage in my pocket, dig out her Christmas present and place it on the table in front of her.

She takes another drag and exhales immediately, her eyes fixed on a spot under the table. She says exactly what I expected her to say. Exactly nothing.

'Merry Christmas everyone,' I shout, my arms raised above my head like a footballer acknowledging the home crowd, and slowly shuffle towards the door. 'And a happy New fucking Year.'

It's cold outside, the cars stretched and sealed with a layer of frost, and I realise that I've left my overcoat inside.

But I can't go back in to get it.

'There's no going back,' I tell myself out loud but I'm not sure what I mean by that right now. In the morning I might.

# Epilogue

I'm not usually nervous about flying. Being nervous never made any sense to me. But I am this time. Or at least I was until I had a few stiffs one. They steadied me down nicely and calmed a stomach craving reassurance after a night on the tiles. Another night on the tiles.

It's been like that since Christmas. Since Clare broke off diplomatic relations to be exact. Then there was that Christmas party the week after, the one they're still talking about. Then there was a few days in Cork. Then a few more in West Cork with Jimmy, who was home for the holiday. We even found that hovel where I had my stag. I'd never have found it or wanted to. But Jimmy did. Trust Jimmy.

January was more sobering, to begin with anyway. Danaher had me in his office at ten past nine on the first day back and I knew in advance that at least one of his New Year resolutions concerned me. I had a tip-off that he was going to try and offload me for once and for all.

I could guess the reasons he'd give to his betters. Public brawl. Shoddy work. Personal problems. Bad for morale. Fresh start. Best all round.

But I saved him the bother. Told him I had decided to take the package the bank had been waving under our noses for the past year and to make myself scarce.

So there, you smug git.

His face was a picture. Two pictures really. Relieved that I had saved him the paperwork but pissed that he didn't have the satisfaction of having me transferred to an inner-city drugzone or some midlands *gulag* where they still bless themselves when passing churches.

'Have you plans?' He looked concerned. Expression No. 47 from the book of Caring Expressions For The Two-Faced. It didn't work, he just looked curious instead.

'None. None at all,' I lied.

I've only told Matt, which means that Clare has an inkling that something's afoot too. But only that. An inkling. I would have told her by now, except that she refuses to acknowledge my existence any more. I've become The Invisible Man. She looks right through me.

I've seen her twice since Wing-Mirror Saturday and we didn't exchange as much as a grunted greeting either day. The first time I called to give Matt his Christmas present and she was in the kitchen doing the ironing and listening to the radio, humming along to The Divine Comedy.

> *Everybody knows that I love you*
> *Everybody knows that I need you . . .*

She didn't even look up. A man's coat was casually draped over the banister as if it belonged there. Maybe it did.

When I called over last weekend she made a point of not answering the door, although she was in the hall getting Matt ready when I rang the bell. When he kissed her goodbye, we were only a few feet apart on the doorstep. Still nothing.

It was the weekend of that eagerly anticipated trip to

Anfield and Matt was all a dither because he couldn't find his red scarf. It would have been a perfect opportunity for small talk but she decided not to take it.

I was polite and said goodbye but she just shut the door quietly. So be it.

Somewhere between the match and a stroll around the Albert Docks I told Matt that I was going away. Not too far and not for too long but just until things settled down. Whatever that meant. It was no big deal I told him and it isn't either. I made him promise not to tell.

He just shrugged his shoulders, said fine and let it at that. He seems to shrug at everything these days. So do I, as it happens. Like father, like son.

I hope that shrug was as insignificant as it looked. Hope that he didn't cry himself to sleep that night, his head buried in the pillow. If I worry about anything, I worry about that. It hasn't been too awful for him up to now, knowing that I was only a short drive away. Knowing that I was there when he needed me in a hurry. Not that he ever did or would have admitted to it.

He used to ring all right. Sometimes on a Monday or Wednesday night after he'd listened to a big game on Five Live. Clare wasn't supposed to know he was making those calls because they were after lights out, so he used to whisper down the line. A few calls ended abruptly when he was tumbled. Caught by the headmistress.

I'll miss that and I suppose he will. I used to stay in just in case he called and was a bit put out when he didn't.

I'll miss our Saturdays too. The odd hike up the mountains. The kickabouts. He was Michael Owen. I had to do with being the hatchetman whose tackles were always late. Penalty. Yellow card.

I'll miss the cheek and the back answers too. The pouts even.

But sneaked phone calls and a few overcrowded hours together were never enough. They didn't mean I was rearing him or even contributing much. I couldn't make a life out of them. I couldn't hang around all week just so I could spend a half-day pretending that everything was fine.

Everything wasn't fine. Everything was terrible. This flight is the start of putting things right. For Matt too. Eventually. Hopefully.

It's not as if I'm abandoning him or turning my back on him and giving up. I couldn't do that. Never would. I'm just taking a breather. Taking time out. I have to. I realise that now. Jimmy made me realise it. Forced me to recognise it.

Sipping hot ones in a Schull pub he told me that I could turn the whole mess on its head and make an opportunity out of it.

We weren't pissed at the time, just thawing out after a gruelling five-hour hike along the coast which was into the face of an unrelenting and biting Atlantic gale.

'Face it, Dan. By your own admission, you and Clare are history; your boss has you by the short and curlies and then there's that Sinead mess. If I were you, I'd cut my losses.'

'Like how?'

'Like get out. Quit. Fuck off. Do the States by Grey-hound. Go on safari. Take the shag express to Bangkok.'

'I can't just scarper like that.' But even as I was saying these words I realised that I could.

I've realised since that I had only been waiting for

someone to tell me to get up off my arse and down from the cross. Someone to tell me that I wasn't obliged to keep revisiting the scene of a car crash that nearly wrecked my life. Clare had moved on. Now I was entitled to move on too.

I spent a few sleepless nights sitting up in bed chain-smoking and a few more afterwards, tossing and turning, before I really began to believe I could do it. That I could pack my bag and leave.

It took me another week to round up the stray ifs and buts.

And here I am. There's no going back now and nothing to go back to. Not even the Beetle. It's gone. Sold. It was the new wing mirror that swung the deal. No mistake.

Not that I'm doing the States by bus or bagging game in Kenya. Not my thing at all. I'm just heading to London. I have a few months of contract work lined up with NatWest and I'll take it from there. They love white-collar Micks over there now. Can't get enough of us.

Jimmy was delighted when I rang to ask if I could stay over at his place for a while. Surprised too, I think. Reckoned I didn't have the bottle. I have, or at least I think so.

We're well on our way now and I could do with another drink. I'm feeling edgy again, can't seem to relax. The *Guardian* reader next to me has slipped me a few curious glances. He must think that I'm one of those jittery fliers. But it's not that; I'm just a little anxious about what happens to me when we land. And then what happens next after that.

It's only natural.

Memories start to intrude. Unwelcome and uninvited

ones from another life. God only knows what brought them on. They're from a life that I inhabited with Clare and Matt. That life. Before it went bad. Simple things parade across my head in a jumbled collage of images. Ordinary things. Walks. Meals. Birthdays. Holidays. Stuff like that. Lots and lots of them.

I don't even have a single photograph of that other life with me. Not even a picture of Matt in my wallet. My wedding ring is gone too. I threw it into the sea at Schull when I was very drunk and it seemed the thing to do.

I find a tissue and blow my nose. My mouth feels dry and my brow feels sticky. Could be that I'm coming down with something or the air conditioning isn't working properly but it's probably neither. It's more than likely just me. I need to a get hold of things. Take charge.

Deep breath. In. Deep. Out. Slowly. And again. I remember doing that before. Seems an age ago now. It is, if you consider everything that has happened since. Enough for a full lifetime and some leftovers. I was in a vile temper that night. Ready to burst. This time I simply feel afraid. Almost frightened.

It didn't seem scary when we talked it through that day in West Cork. Even during those sleepless nights, being scared wasn't something that came up. Just shows you can't cover all the angles.

I unwrap the headphones from around my Walkman, put on *Rubber Soul* and lean forward to look out the window. The plane tilts slightly and then dips into a wispy shroud of clouds just below. We're nearly there.

I fasten my belt as we begin our steep descent, shut my eyes and listen to 'Norwegian Wood'.

When I open them again the song will be over, we'll have landed and I won't be scared any more.

That's the plan anyway.